MORTIMER SAYS NOTHING

A CHARLOTTE ZOLOTOW BOOK

Joan Aiken

MORTIMER SAYS NOTHING

Containing

Mortimer Says Nothing
Arabel's Birthday
Mr. Jones's Rest Cure
A Call at the Joneses'

Illustrated by Quentin Blake

1 8 1 7

HARPER & ROW, PUBLISHERS

Cambridge, Philadelphia, San Francisco, Washington, London, Mexico City, São Paolo, Singapore, Sydney

NEW YORK

To Quentin Blake

Mortimer Says Nothing
Published in Great Britain by Jonathan Cape
Copyright © 1985 by Joan Aiken Enterprises Ltd
All rights reserved. No part of this book may be
used or reproduced in any manner whatsoever without
written permission except in the case of brief quotations
embodied in critical articles and reviews. Printed in
the United States of America. For information address
Harper & Row Junior Books, 10 East 53rd Street,
New York, N.Y. 10022.

10 9 8 7 6 5 4 3 2 1

First American Edition

Library of Congress Cataloging-in-Publication Data
Aiken, Joan, 1924–
    Mortimer says nothing.

    Reprint. Originally published: London: J. Cape,
c 1985.
    "A Charlotte Zolotow book."
    Summary: Four adventures of Arabel and her pet
raven Mortimer: "Mortimer Says Nothing," "Arabel's
Birthday," "Mr. Jones's Rest Cure," and "A Call at the
Joneses'."
    [1. Ravens—Fiction. 2. Humorous stories] I. Blake,
Quentin, ill. II. Title.
PZ7.A2695Mor 1987   [Fic]   86-45488
ISBN 0-06-020038-3
ISBN 0-06-020039-1 (lib. bdg.)

CONTENTS

MORTIMER SAYS NOTHING

It was on the day when Mrs. Jones heard that the ladies of Rumbury Town were coming to visit her kitchen that the mice of Cantilever Green began their march north across London.

Both these things happened at about the same time, but we will tell about Mrs. Jones first.

The news about the ladies of Rumbury Town broke while the Jones family were at breakfast. Mr. Jones was bolting down his scrambled eggs very fast, for he was a taxi driver and had been booked to take a fare (actually it was his friend and neighbor Mr. MacDoritch) all the way to Scotland to see Mr. MacDoritch's son Dougal toss the caber in some Highland Games. Mr. Jones would be away from home for one night, maybe two.

Mortimer, the family raven, was gazing at the pepper grinder, with which Mr. Jones had just finished peppering his scrambled eggs. When nobody was watching him, Mortimer unscrewed the top of the grinder and peered inside it. He saw a hole, a metal pin going down into the hole, and a quantity of peppercorns. Quietly,

Mortimer tipped the grinder upside down and swallowed all the peppercorns.

Then, as an afterthought, he swallowed the top of the grinder.

After that, he climbed onto the back of Arabel's chair and sat there looking pensive.

Arabel Jones, who was small and fair and very well behaved, was eating cornflakes.

Mrs. Jones was reading a postcard from Auntie Winnie at Portmadoc.

" 'Having a lovely time, wish you were here,' Auntie Winnie says," Mrs. Jones read out. She took a bite of toast and opened her other letter, which was in a fancy pink-and-brown deckle-edged envelope. When she saw what was typed on the single sheet inside, she turned white as frozen pastry and let out a wail.

"Oh, my stars! Oh, *no*! Oh, whatever shall I *do*? Oh, mercy! And I just sent the yellow-and-dusty-pink coordinated kitchen curtains to the cleaners. And the toasted sandwich maker keeps turning out the sandwiches inside out. And the manually controlled flow regulator on the coffeepot has gone funny. And all the cast-iron cookware wants processing with vegetable oil. And the copper-and-Teflon wants polishing. And the infrared grill's gone infragreen! And my new mail-order wooden dessert dishes from Happy-Pliances haven't come yet, nor has the Bijou Cuisinette. And Mortimer ate the stone breadboard last Thursday, drat him! And all the houseplants have got Houseplant's Knee!"

"Kaaark!" said Mortimer in a melancholy tone. He

was remembering that, sad to tell, he had not enjoyed the stone breadboard. Mortimer liked almost all forms of food. He could swallow anything, from an umbrella to an electric iron. He was very pleased with the warming effect the peppercorns were having inside him now. But the stone breadboard *had* been a mistake. It had been heavy and indigestible, and tasted of nothing in particular. Also, for days after, Mortimer found climbing the stairs unusually hard work.

"Oh, Ben," lamented Mrs. Jones, "you'll just *have* to fix the flow regulator on the coffeepot before you go. And the infrared grill. And the toasted sandwich maker."

"What are you going on about, Martha?" said Mr. Jones, looking at his watch.

"The Rumbury Ladies' Kitchen Club!"

"Who the deuce are they, pray, when they're at home?"

"They practically never *are* at home!"

"Who are they?" patiently repeated Mr. Jones.

"Oh, *you* know, Ben! I've been a member for ever so long. We all pay each other visits—every week all the ladies pay a visit to one of the other ladies in their kitchens—"

"Hold on. Who visits who, in whose kitchen?"

"It's a different kitchen every week," said Mrs. Jones, hiccuping distractedly. "And the lady who's selected as that week's hostess serves tea and coffee and cakes and sandwiches and mouth-watering snacks in her kitchen, and all the other ladies partake! And of course they all poke into everything and ask why you don't have a Blendmaster with an electronic memory, and what happens when the cat gets down your sink destructor unit, and why you don't use the ejector on your crumble machine, and what is your recipe for Icelandic Persimmon Cake. And, if your coffee isn't as good as the coffee the week before, the news is all over Rumbury Town in a flash. And this week they've selected *me* as hostess! It says so, right here! 'The Rainwater Crescent Branch of the Rumbury Ladies' Kitchen Club has honored you by electing you as this week's Hostess. At Home Day will be August 28. We shall be pleased to join you in your kitchen at 11:30 A.M. Estimated number of guests will be thirty.' Oh, how can I ever manage to get the coordinated curtains back from the cleaners in time! 'If you would prefer to serve a light luncheon, please check

Box A,' it says. Oh, Ben, you *will* repair the infrared grill and the sandwich maker and the manually controlled flow on the coffee machine before you go, won't you?"

" 'Fraid not, Martha. I've got to go now, this minute," said Mr. Jones, hastily gulping down the last of his tea and standing up. " 'Check Box A,' what cheek," he muttered to himself. "Light luncheon, indeed! I'd give 'em a light luncheon they'd remember! Thank goodness I'll be in Scotland, most likely. I can't think why you belong to this barmy club."

"Oh, but it's ever so nice, Ben! I've had ever so many morning coffees in other ladies' kitchens, and ever such interesting times afterward, discussing what they did wrong. Oh, my cats alive, how shall I ever bear it now it's my turn? I've a good mind to resign now, right away."

"Then they'd all say your kitchen must be a horrible mess," pointed out Mr. Jones warningly, wrapping himself up in a long muffler because he was sure it would be cold in Scotland. He gave his daughter Arabel a kiss. "You be a good girl now, Arabel, dearie, and help your Mum, and don't let that bird get up to mischief," and he threw a sharp glance at Mortimer, who was now rocking slowly back and forth, to allow the warmth from the peppercorns to trickle all around inside him.

Mrs. Jones agreed mournfully. "I reckon you're right, Ben. I'll have to have the ladies here. Maybe I'd better make some of my macaroons and meringues."

"That's the ticket," said Mr. Jones heartily. "Your meringues and macaroons are champion. I bet they don't

make 'em any better at the Hollywood Hilton. Well, so long," said Mr. Jones, putting on his thickest cap. "I'll bring you back a haggis from Scotland."

"But, Ben! What about the infrared grill—and the manually controlled flow—?"

"Make the ladies their coffee in a jug," suggested Mr. Jones. "Or ask Sid Smith to fix them—if he has the time—" and he hastily kissed his wife and went out to his taxi, which was parked in front of the house in Rainwater Crescent.

Meanwhile the mice of Cantilever Green, which is an area of London some ten kilometers southwest of Rumbury Town, were holding an emergency meeting.

"Friends," said the chairmouse, "we have to face this problem: there is no more food in this place. Sad, grieved though we shall be to leave our homeland, the land of our forefathers, our duty is plain. Our wives and children are starving. So are we. Fate is driving us onward. We must shoulder the pioneer's burden and travel to new parts."

"Hear, hear!" shouted the rest of the mice, who were all thin, hungry, and bad tempered, for it was true, they had eaten every scrap of food in Cantilever Green. "Which way shall we go?"

"We must elect a scout, to prospect and spy out the land."

So a scout was elected. His name was Senior Scout F Stroke B7 Popeye.

"You must travel fast," the chairmouse told him, "for our need is urgent."

It was indeed. Cantilever Green had been quite cleared out by the mice. Supermarkets had been emptied, corner grocers denuded, cake shops devastated, homes, bakers, and cafeterias cleaned of their last crumb. In fact, the Cantilever Green Health Department was about to start using tear gas, mustard bombs, and hot-water hoses on the mice, so it was time for them to go.

Senior Scout F Stroke B7 was ordered to travel northward.

"Don't try Fulham or Chelsea," warned the chairmouse. "I know for a fact they have strong mouse-protection defense leagues there. And Westminster is no good, for it's full of cats. Look farther away. Highgate, or Finchley, or Rumbury Town. The air up there should be good for our children, too."

Scout F Stroke B7 promised to do his best for the tribe, and started out, traveling at top speed. He was a

shrewd and experienced hitchhiker, making expert use of strollers, shopping carts, girls' trailing skirts, umbrellas, briefcases, and the London Transport bus and underground system. By lunchtime he had reached Rainwater Crescent, Rumbury Town, where he nosed his way along through the back gardens, sniffing, prospecting, and testing the air.

At 1345 hours he effected an entry into the pantry of Number Six, Rainwater Crescent, which was the home of the Jones family. The reason why he selected this particular house was the very delicious smell of hot, crisp macaroons that came wafting out through the pantry window.

F Stroke B7 climbed up the Virginia creeper and in no time had nibbled his way through the wooden window frame and was sitting inside on the sill, looking down like stout Cortez on an ocean of macaroons.

They were spread out to cool on wire mesh trays: hundreds of them.

F Stroke B7 sampled half a dozen, and found them first class. In all his life he had never eaten better quality, and he decided to report very favorably to his committee on the amenities of Rumbury Town. There seemed no point in going on any farther. I'll wait here till dark, he thought, and then go back and tell the folk at home that the food supply in Rumbury Town is quite up to our required standard. Meanwhile I'll just sample a few more macaroons. . . .

After nibbling another half dozen, F Stroke B7 fell asleep, curled up comfortably in a custard tart, from which he had first carefully removed the custard.

Meanwhile Mrs. Jones was having a good deal of trouble with her mixers.

She had three of these. Her favorite was a little old

Polish one, which Mr. Jones had brought her back a long, long time ago, when he was a sailor in the merchant navy, from some port in the Baltic. It was like a metal prong with a little windmill at one end and a tiny electric motor in the handle. Unfortunately she had had it so long and used it so much that it was becoming worn out. As well as this, she had a hand electric blender gotten by mail order from Happy-Pliances, Ltd., which had two prongs that worked like an eggbeater; and she had a similar one, bought off a stall in Copernicus Road street market, which had two small plastic whizzers and a long plastic attachment like an upside-down castle. As well as these she had a big automatic blender. But she didn't like any of them so well as her little old Polish one.

Making meringues entails beating a whole lot of eggs, and by the time Mrs. Jones had beaten enough eggs to make two hundred meringues, her little old Polish mixer was red hot, and letting out blue smoke. As she mixed the last batch, it broke down entirely; with one last expiring crackle, it stopped beating.

"Oh, heavens, whatever shall I do now?" said Mrs. Jones.

"Maybe Mr. Smith will mend it for you, Ma," said Arabel.

"I daren't ask him to mend anything else," said Mrs. Jones. "He's already got the coffee machine and the sandwich maker and the grill. I'll just have to make do with my other mixers, or the automatic, though I don't like them half so well."

Mrs. Jones went into the pantry to get some more eggs. She had just picked up a box of six when she noticed Scout F Stroke B7 curled up fast asleep in the empty custard-tart case. She let out a piercing shriek and dropped the eggs on the tiled floor. They all broke.

Arabel and Mortimer came hurrying to see what was the matter with Mrs. Jones. At least Arabel hurried; Mortimer seldom moved fast. He walked slowly across the tiles, trod in a puddle of egg white, slid, and sat down on his tail. Slithery egg white got in among his feathers. Mortimer did not object to this; indeed he rather enjoyed the sensation. He began eating up the yolks of eggs and bits of shell that were scattered about the kitchen floor.

"What happened, Ma?" asked Arabel.

By now Scout F Stroke B7 was not to be seen. Roused by Mrs. Jones's shriek, he had taken cover, rather unwisely, inside an electric toaster that stood on the pantry shelf. Luckily the toaster was not plugged in.

"There was a mouse! I saw a mouse!" wailed Mrs. Jones. "There has never, *ever* been a mouse in this house, not since I can remember! Not since Coronation year! Not since Granny Jones stayed with us and bought that hat with the grapes on it. Oh, why does this have to happen *now,* just answer me that?"

"I don't know, Ma," said Arabel. "Shall I fetch the mousetrap?"

"No, it's in the toaster," said Mrs. Jones, which puzzled Arabel until her mother picked up the toaster and began to carry it across the kitchen toward the back door. She meant to take it into the garden and empty the mouse out there, but unfortunately she, too, stepped on a slippery patch of egg white. She slid, recovered herself, but dropped the toaster. Scout F Stroke B7 bounced out onto the kitchen floor. Very sensibly, he made a dash for the gas stove and nipped in behind it.

"Oh, drabbit it!" said Mrs. Jones. "That stove's too heavy for me to shift. Arabel, dearie, run up to the corner shop, will you, and get me another dozen eggs, and ask Mrs. Catchpenny if she will kindly lend us Archibald."

"Mortimer won't like that," said Arabel.

Archibald was Mrs. Catchpenny's cat.

"We can't run our lives to suit that bird," snapped

Mrs. Jones, wiping up egg white with a floor cloth. "He must learn to take the rough with the smooth, like the rest of us."

"Nevermore," murmured Mortimer, raising his wings to enjoy the sticky feel of egg white in among his feathers. Just at the moment, so far as he was concerned, his life seemed to be mostly smooth. He was having a good time, in his own fashion.

"You'd best take Mortimer with you," added Mrs. Jones. "I don't want him under my feet while I'm trying to clear up this mess of eggs."

"He might catch the mouse for you," suggested Arabel.

"Not him! He never did anything useful in his life."

This was hardly fair of Mrs. Jones, for Mortimer had eaten up nearly all the broken eggs. However, Arabel got out her dolls' stroller and put Mortimer in it. He enjoyed being wheeled along the street, and gazed about him with interest as she walked up to Mrs. Catchpenny's shop at the corner of Rainwater Crescent.

Mrs. Catchpenny wore bedroom slippers all day. They were trodden down at the heels. She always had a cigarette dangling from the corner of her mouth, and her voice was deep and rusty, as if she had been gargling with water that old nails had been soaked in. Her shop sold milk, butter, tea, coffee, soap, cans of things, cheese, eggs, birthday cards, newspapers, cauliflowers, frozen peas, hooks, clothespins, matches, and almost anything else you can think of.

"Hello, dear," said Mrs. Catchpenny, in her deep voice,

when Arabel pushed open the door, which had a bell that pinged. "Your Ma's busy today, isn't she? What can I do you for this time?"

"A dozen large eggs, please," said Arabel. "And here's the money, and Ma says, please may we borrow Archibald?"

Archibald had been a stray kitten when he fell down Mrs. Catchpenny's chimney. Mrs. Catchpenny took a fancy to him, decided to keep him, and fed him on condensed milk and anchovies. Now he was grown full size, and could fight any cat in Rumbury Town with two paws tied behind his back. He was black, with green eyes, and had won first prize, in the class for strays, at several local cat shows. He was said to be a champion mouser.

" 'Course you can borrow him, dearie," said Mrs. Catchpenny. "Got a mouse, have you? Archibald'll soon settle his hash—won't you, lovie?"

Archibald was sitting on the counter beside the chocolate sesame bars, with his tail tucked round his paws. He was almost as big as Arabel, and was looking in a decidedly unfriendly manner at Mortimer, who glared back, as if for two pins he'd chop Archibald's tail off.

"It's best not to cross him," warned Mrs. Catchpenny. "Archibald can be a holy terror when he's crossed. He got left in the country once, when me and my hubby took him on a picnic, and he got out of the car, and we didn't notice he was missing till we got home."

"What happened?" asked Arabel.

"We'd stopped at pubs in several places, so we didn't know where he might be. And it took two days to find him, driving about. But when we *did* find him, there he was, sitting by the roadside, just boiling with temper. He took a chunk right out of my hubby's leg. And the farmer who owned the land said no one could get near him in those two days—not dogs nor cows nor pigs nor policemen nor people. He just fought them off. He was going to stay on that spot till we came for him—and then he was going to give us what for."

"Do you think he'll come with me?" Arabel asked rather doubtfully, and she called, "Puss, Puss," in a polite tone. Archibald shut his eyes and took no notice at all.

"He might come with you if you tempted him with an anchovy," said Mrs. Catchpenny, and she levered an anchovy out of a can that lay open on the counter. But Archibald had just eaten a large lunch and was not interested. So Mrs. Catchpenny shunted her cigarette farther into the corner of her mouth, walked to the end of the shop, and called "Lil!" loudly up the stairs.

"What?" said a bored voice from above.

"Mind the shop for a couple minutes, will you, while I take Archibald to the Joneses'?"

"OK," said the bored voice, and the noise of a transistor and steps started down the stairs.

Mrs. Catchpenny hoisted up Archibald under one arm, where he dangled, head and feet down like a sack of potatoes. Mrs. Catchpenny slip-slopped in her trodden-down slippers, around the Crescent to the Joneses' house. Arabel pattered along beside, pushing the dolls' stroller with Mortimer in it, and carrying the eggs in a plastic bag.

Archibald did not struggle or scratch, but growled

gently to himself in a deep voice so like Mrs. Catchpenny's that Arabel would not have been surprised to see a cigarette dangling from his mouth too. Mrs. Catchpenny carried his can of anchovies in her other hand.

"Just to make him feel at home," she said. "And I wouldn't let him near that bird of yours. Or you'll have nothing left but feathers."

"I think Mortimer can look after himself," said Arabel. "But if they don't seem to get on, I'll shut him in my bedroom." She thought this might be best for Archibald too.

"There you are, then, love," said Mrs. Catchpenny to Mrs. Jones, pouring Archibald like a jugful of tar onto the kitchen floor, which was now clean and washed. "Got a mouse, have you? Archibald'll have it trussed and stuffed before you can say Merry Christmas!"

"Oh, that's ever so kind of you, dear," said Mrs. Jones. "The mouse went behind the stove and I haven't seen it since."

In fact Scout F Stroke B7 had left the Joneses' house a long time ago. He seized the chance to slip out the front door when Arabel went out with Mortimer. But Mrs. Jones, busy mopping the floor, had not noticed this.

Mrs. Catchpenny pointed Archibald toward the stove like a rocket. He sniffed around the stove in a bored, leisurely manner, shrugged, if a cat can shrug, jumped onto a pile of clean dust cloths, and went to sleep.

"That probably means it's gone down its hole," said Mrs. Catchpenny. "He'll snap it up fast enough when it shows its face, don't you worry. Now," she said to Archibald, "don't you come home till you've caught that mouse, my boy." Archibald shrugged again, keeping his eyes shut, burying his nose deeper in his tail. "I'll put the anchovies by him," said Mrs. Catchpenny, and did. "Got company coming then?" she inquired, noticing the twenty bun pans full of cake mixture, forty scones cool-

ing on a pastry rack, and a huge pudding bowl full of
egg yolks.

"Company! I should just about think I have!" cried
Mrs. Jones, and explained about the Rumbury Ladies'
Kitchen Club.

" 'Struth! I'm glad I'm not in your shoes, dearie! I
wouldn't have any of those old tabbies in my place, not
if each one had a diamond on the end of her nose! Well,
you keep Archibald just as long as you like; he won't
budge so long as you keep feeding him anchovies and
a drop of condensed milk now and then. You won't have
to worry about mice while he's in the place."

"That's ever such a weight off my mind, dear, thanks
ever so," said Mrs. Jones, distractedly fetching a tub of
frozen prawns from the big freezer in the pantry.

"Prawn savories, you going to give 'em?" inquired Mrs.
Catchpenny interestedly.

"No, you see I've got all these egg yolks left over from
the whites I used for the macaroons and meringues,
so I thought I'd make mayonnaise and give the ladies
prawn and radish cocktails, because Arabel's grown ever
such a lot of radishes, haven't you, dear?" said Mrs.
Jones.

"Rather you than me," said Mrs. Catchpenny, and she
slip-slopped away, leaving a trail of cigarette ash across
Mrs. Jones's kitchen floor.

"Shall I wipe the custard glasses, Ma?" said Arabel.

"Before you do that, dearie, just run along to Mrs.
Cross, will you, there's a love, and ask if I can borrow
her big bun pan?"

"Yes, Ma," said Arabel, and she wheeled out Mortimer in the stroller once more.

Coming back along Rainwater Crescent, with Mortimer sitting on the big silver bun pan, which was balanced across the top of the stroller, they met an elderly man who was holding a microphone in front of a sparrow. The sparrow was sitting on Mrs. Smith's front-garden privet hedge, and was saying "Cheep, cheep." The elderly man, who was bald and had big ears and gold-rimmed glasses, was recording what the sparrow said. He had a neat little tape recorder the size of a cricket ball.

"Nevermore!" remarked Mortimer, greatly interested. At this, the bald-headed man spun around very fast. "Good gracious, my dear young child! Did I hear your bird say 'Nevermore'?" He had a slight foreign accent.

"Yes, he did," said Arabel. "He often does."

"But this is magnificent! This is formidable! This is one for my collection! *Also gut, très bien, va bene,*" the bald man said, waving his arms impatiently at the sparrow. "I have done with you, fly away, *por favor, alsdublieft.* Go!" The sparrow flew away.

"I am Professor Glibchick, from the European Institute of Ornitho-Musicological Studies in Freiherrburg," the bald man said to Arabel. "I am here in England to make a collection of British bird vocabulary in syllabic order."

Arabel hadn't the least idea what he was talking about.

"Excuse me, I have to get home because my mother is in a hurry for this bun pan," she said politely. "Also

I am not allowed to talk to strangers in the street."

"Very right, very right! But I shall come to talk to your good mother and she will permit me, I am sure, to make a recording of your excellent bird here."

Mortimer kept silent, his little black eyes like boot buttons attentively watching the professor. He seemed to be enjoying a private joke. Professor Glibchick walked excitedly along the Crescent beside Arabel, explaining about his collection of birdcalls.

"A one-syllable call is most common, as you would expect," he said. "The dove: 'coo.' The duck: 'quack.' The sparrow (as you have just heard): 'cheep.' And, suchwise, many two-syllable calls are most often also heard. The cuckoo, for example: 'cuckoo.' The great tit, which (as you will be aware) is heard to utter 'Tea—cher! Tea—cher!' And there is also the nuthatch, always to be recognized by its call: 'Be quick! Be quick!' "

"Oh?" said Arabel.

"Kaaark," said Mortimer softly.

Professor Glibchick looked disappointed.

"But that bird of yours (a raven if I am not mistaken), I just now distinctly overheard him to say *'Nevermore'*! Three syllables! Which is exceedingly rare—unheard of!"

"Is it?" said Arabel.

"Indeed, indeed yes! A call of three syllables, such as 'Nevermore,' is, my dear child, somewhat unknown!"

"Fancy," said Arabel. She opened the door of Number Six and went in.

"Good day, good day, my dear Madam," said Professor Glibchick, rapidly following Arabel into the kitchen. "I do hope, I do trust, that I do not intrude, that you will permit me to be recording your fine bird?"

"Recording?" said Mrs. Jones. She looked hot and flustered. "Did you get the big bun pan, Arabel, dearie? You'll have to excuse me, I'm sure," she said to the professor. "I'm ever so busy cooking, and I haven't time for any of those Poll Parrot Gallops, or whatever it is you may be doing. Why don't you go along to Mrs. Brown at Number Eight? She always has plenty of time for minding other people's business."

"Please, please do not let me disturb your work. Madam," said Professor Glibchick. "I merely wish to make a tape of your handsome bird saying 'Nevermore.' "

"Well, I'm sure I don't know why you should want to do *that*," said Mrs. Jones. "Measure him, you mean?" She took the bun pan from Arabel and began to rub it with greased paper.

"A trisyllabic call is very rare, very rare indeed, Madam! You have the quadrosyllabic—as, for example, the owl's 'Tu-whit, tu-whoo.' You have the quintosyllabic, as, for instance, the wood pigeon, 'I *do* like porridge.' "

"But I'm not *making* porridge," said Mrs. Jones, more and more bewildered. She wasn't really paying attention to Professor Glibchick, but just wished he would get out of her kitchen. "Buns, scones, meringues, macaroons, mayonnaise, and prawn cocktails." She picked up the hand blender that she had bought mail order from Happy-Pliances, Ltd., and looked about for the two beaters that, when stuck into its front, would turn it into an eggbeater.

Unfortunately Mortimer had quietly swallowed both of them before leaving for Mrs. Catchpenny's shop.

"The thrush," continued Professor Glibchick, "will give us another example of a four-syllable call. 'Did he do it? Did he do it?' "

"Did *who* do *what?*" said Mrs. Jones rather impatiently. "If you mean, did Mortimer swallow my beaters, yes, I daresay he did. I'm sure I don't know where they can have got to otherwise. They were here just now."

"Perhaps I might interview your raven in another room?" suggested the professor, seeing that Mrs. Jones was not inclined to be sympathetic to his work.

But Mrs. Jones had cleaned up the front room all tidy and polished for the Rumbury Ladies, and said she didn't want Mortimer in there getting up to mischief.

"Then I will just put myself in this corner," said Professor Glibchick, seating himself on a kitchen stool. "And the instant your bird resumes his utterance I will record it and remove myself without delay."

Mortimer kept quiet. His little black eyes sparkled.

"Oh, very well!" said Mrs. Jones crossly. "If you must, you must! Dear knows, Mortimer's not usually one to sit with his beak shut for long at a time."

She was whizzing away with her mail-order blender at a bowl of egg white, but she had fitted the blender with the plastic beaters from the mixer she had bought in Copernicus Road street market, and it was doing a very slow job. "Pass me the icing sugar, will you, Arabel, dearie, and fetch the old hand eggbeater out of the drawer? I can't think why this egg white is taking such a long time to whip."

Professor Glibchick sat staring at Mortimer, holding the microphone ten centimeters from his beak. And Mortimer stared back in silence, keeping his beak resolutely shut. For once he did not seem inclined to speak.

He knew perfectly well that the professor wanted him to. And he was in a teasing mood.

"I should be obliged, Madam," said the professor, "if—supposing your raven *does* decide to discourse— you would be so kind as to switch off some of your machines, or my recorder will hardly be able to pick up his words."

There was certainly a good deal of noise in the kitchen. The big automatic blender was working on its own, chopping radishes and parsley. The kitchen refrigerator hummed loudly to itself because Mrs. Jones had switched it to Extra Cold. The oven timer was warbling to let Mrs. Jones know that another batch of scones was ready to come out. The whistling kettle was whistling its head off. Also, not quite so loud, Archibald the cat was snoring as he lay stretched, in another corner, on his pile of dust cloths, with his anchovy can beside him. He was deep, deep asleep. Every now and then his nose, paws, and tail would twitch a little. He was dreaming about mice.

Everyone had forgotten him, even Mortimer.

Meanwhile, what about the mice of Cantilever Green?

At this very moment they were receiving a report from their brave Scout F Stroke B7 Popeye, who had traveled at terrific speed back to his home territory; he had been lucky in hopping a lift on the fur coat of an old lady who took a taxi from Rumbury Town to Knitting Dell High Street, which is only half a kilometer from Cantilever Green. And the last half kilometer was swiftly achieved by clinging to the underside of a shaggy Russian deerhound who was chasing a Jack Russell terrier. Scout F Stroke B7 was able to swing himself down within twenty meters of the Cantilever Green mouse headquarters, which was in a disused nursery school.

"Friends! Just listen to this! Rumbury Town is a land of milk and honey!" cried F Stroke B7 enthusiastically to the assembled thin and hungry mice of Cantilever Green. "Why, in one single domestic pantry in Rainwater Crescent I counted three hundred macaroons, eighty scones, one hundred and twenty-three queen cakes, and evident signs that more delicacies were in preparation. If they have all that in one private house, only imagine what the cake shops and restaurants must be like!"

"But what about the local hazards?" asked the chairmouse. "What about cats, dogs, owls, eagles, hawks, foxes, weasels, and mousetraps?"

"There were none to be seen. The single thing approaching a hazard that I observed was a raven. But at the time I observed him he was eating the beaters of an electric mixer. It is my belief that ravens who eat eggbeaters do not eat mice."

The mice of Cantilever Green were greatly impressed by this statement. (In fact, long after the migration to Rumbury Town had passed into history and mouse legend, the proverb "Ravens who eat eggbeaters won't touch mice" was remembered and quoted. "But what does it mean?" young mice sometimes asked, and their elders would say wisely, "Ah, when you are old and experienced, you will understand," and shake their whiskers with a knowledgeable air.)

"Well, comrades," said the chairmouse, "what is your

decision? Shall we act on the report of our brave Scout F Stroke B7? Shall we move to Rumbury Town?"

"Aye! Aye! Carried unanimouse-ly! Let us set off at once!" shouted the famished mice; and before the chair-mouse could even put it to a vote, they were busily packing up their little bundles of dried-grass matting and other household goods, preparing to set out on their perilous journey.

Of course it takes longer for a whole urban district full of mice to travel ten kilometers than it does for a single expert and resourceful courier. Most of the Cantilever Green tribe, and all the women and children, had to wait and do their traveling by night; they could not risk being seen in their thousands crossing Holland Park

Avenue or scurrying around Marble Arch. But still, split into parties of a hundred for extra safety, and taking different routes, they managed to keep up a good pace, helped by some cooperative bats, who flew overhead, like traffic helicopters, with warnings about dangers ahead, and suggestions as to shortcuts.

Meanwhile Mrs. Jones, working harder than the Egyptians who built the pyramids, using her hand eggbeater, had made an enormous number of meringues from egg white and sugar, and had put them in the upstairs airing cupboard to harden off. The airing cupboard was always warm; it was exactly right for hardening off meringues. It was also exactly right (or so *he* thought) for Mortimer; he loved getting in there and sitting with his feathers fluffed out among the clean sheets and towels. Mrs. Jones did not approve of this; in fact, only last week she had got Mr. Jones to put a new latch on the door, with a burglar-proof lock and a tiny key, which was kept hanging on a separate hook by the door. Up to now, this had kept Mortimer out of the cupboard; he had not found the key.

Professor Glibchick remained in the Jones kitchen for six hours, with his tape recorder, trying to persuade Mortimer to say "Nevermore." But Mortimer, just because for once somebody *wanted* him to speak, had remained most provokingly and disobligingly silent, staring with all his might at the professor, but keeping his beak tight shut, as if he had a golden butterfly trapped inside it. He was enjoying himself hugely; never before had he found *not* making a noise such a pleasure. Mrs. Jones was too harassed and bothered with her cooking to pay much heed to them; she wished the professor would go away, but she could not honestly say that he was much of a nuisance, waiting on his stool, holding the microphone in front of Mortimer.

And Archibald the cat slept on his pile of dust cloths.

At last, late in the evening, the professor left, announcing that he would come back early next morning.

"I suppose I can't stop you," sighed Mrs. Jones, wiping her forehead with a floury hand. "And one thing I will say, sitting and staring at you all day keeps the bird out of mischief. Which I can do with. Oh, my lord! When I think of those ladies coming the day after tomorrow, it makes my heart bang against my persiflage!"

Mrs. Jones and Arabel retired to bed, quite tired out, Mrs. Jones with making scones, cakes, buns, and meringues, Arabel with polishing all the knives, teaspoons, salad forks, and sugar tongs, besides folding hundreds of paper napkins into water lilies, a clever trick she had learned from Auntie Meg in Wales.

Mortimer went quietly and tried the airing-cupboard door. But, finding it locked, he spent the night in the coal scuttle, where the coal dust stuck most comfortably to the gooey egg white under his wings.

Nobody thought to wonder where Archibald the cat would pass the night. In fact, Arabel and her mother were so tired that they never thought about him at all.

Archibald slept on his dust cloths till midnight; then he woke up and finished his anchovies. Then he prowled silently all over the Joneses' house, inspecting it with a professional eye.

In his young days, Archibald had been a burglar's mog, or peter; that is, a burglar's helper. It had been Archibald's job to get into houses through tiny windows, or drainpipes, or down chimneys; then he let in the rest of the gang by undoing locks or bolts on doors or windows. This was how he had gotten into Mrs. Catchpenny's house, down the chimney. But, once inside, he had decided that it would be better to settle down in a place where people were so generous with their anchovies and condensed milk. The gang had abandoned him, thinking he must have gotten stuck in the chimney, though they were sorry to lose a mog who had been trained to open every kind of catch in London.

Having finished his anchovies, and looking for a warmer place to pass the rest of the night, Archibald strolled upstairs. It took him no time at all to undo the latch on the airing-cupboard door; then he pulled the door open with his paw and went inside.

There were four slatted shelves in the cupboard. On three of the shelves Mrs. Jones had put large trays of warm, crisp white meringues. Archibald was not fond of meringues; he never ate sweet things, apart from condensed milk; but the airing cupboard was pleasantly warm, so he stretched himself out along the bottom shelf, on top of the meringues, and went back to sleep. At first the meringues supported his weight, like an air pillow; but Archibald was a heavy cat, and they slowly crumbled and subsided under him, until they were re-

duced to a flat, squashed layer, like the foundation under a house, partly sticky and partly crumbly. When Archibald woke and discovered what had happened, he climbed up to the next shelf and lay down on another batch of meringues. After an hour, this happened again.

On the top shelf of the cupboard was an old down-filled cushion that leaked feathers; Mrs. Jones kept intending to take it to the cleaners on Rumbury High Street who had a pillow-restuffing service. Just before dawn, Archibald climbed right up and found this pillow, which was deliciously comfortable and smelled of birds. He settled down on it for his final nap.

During this time the mice of Cantilever Green had gotten more than halfway on their great overland march, traveling through the night.

They did not stop to eat along the way. "Tighten your belts, brothers!" urged the chairmouse. "Think of the glorious plenty that lies ahead! We can afford to go hungry for one more night. If we don't touch so much as a peanut or a potato chip on the way, nobody will be able to follow our trail. Remember the macaroons that are waiting for us!"

With stomachs rumbling, the mice plodded on. By dawn they had reached the foot of Vicarsbury Hill, only one and a half kilometers from Rumbury Town. They settled down there to pass the day in a disused railway shunting house.

Shortly after dawn, Archibald woke, thinking about breakfast, jumped softly down from the airing-cupboard top shelf, and prowled downstairs. Without the least difficulty he let himself into Mrs. Jones's pantry, where he made a very satisfactory breakfast of ham, fish fingers from the pantry freezer (Archibald preferred fish fingers frozen; he liked to scrunch them), a great many prawns, and a couple of pots of cream. Then shutting the door carefully behind him, he was about to return upstairs for another nap in the airing cupboard when he encountered Mortimer, who had been roused from sleep by the click of the pantry latch.

Mortimer had totally forgotten about the black cat who had been brought into the Joneses' house by Mrs. Catchpenny. Although at the time he had meant to give

Archibald a thrashing, or at least nip his tail off just to show him who was boss at Number Six, Rainwater Crescent, the fun of teasing Professor Glibchick had put the intruder right out of Mortimer's head. And, even if he had remembered Archibald, Mortimer would never have connected the black cat with the creature that he saw on the stairs at dawn. For the soft duck feathers from the molting pillow had clung to Archibald's sticky, meringue-coated fur, and he was covered all over with a thick brownish-gray layer of plumy down, so that he looked like a big shapeless untidy bird, with green eyes, whiskers, and a tail.

"Nevermore!" said Mortimer, really amazed. He took Archibald for some kind of owl, an extra-big one with four feet.

At this point Archibald was on the bottom stair, lazy and sleepy, because he was full of breakfast. Ordinarily he would have wanted to fight Mortimer; but just now he didn't. Mortimer poked his beak inquisitively through the banisters; Archibald swatted the beak with a good-natured paw, and strolled up one step. Mortimer, who was quite tall, then poked his beak between the next pair of banisters, and again Archibald swatted it, climbing up another step. He was feeling playful, being so full of prawns, ham, and cream. Mortimer, also in a sociable mood, began to enjoy the game. He went on climbing the stairs, outside the banisters, hanging on with his claws and poking his beak at Archibald through each gap in turn, while Archibald made feinting darts with his paw, prodding Mortimer in the stomach. When

they got to the top, Mortimer suddenly squeezed through between the rails and hurled himself at Archibald; the two then rolled from the top to the bottom of the stairs, kicking each other, not very seriously. When they reached the bottom, Archibald began licking Mortimer, whose feathers were still packed with coal dust and egg white.

Archibald found this mixture to his taste: rather like farina.

Nobody—not even his mother—had *ever* licked Mortimer before. He enjoyed it hugely. He lay in ecstasy on his back with beak and feet in the air, murmuring "Kaaark" dreamily. Sometimes, when he could reach, he scratched between Archibald's ears with his beak.

After half an hour or so the friends parted. Mortimer went back to his coal scuttle, and Archibald returned to his nest on the top shelf of the airing cupboard, closing the door behind him to keep out drafts.

Mrs. Jones did not look in the airing cupboard when she got up. She knew that her meringues took eighteen hours to dry out and would then be quite perfect. So she hurried herself and Arabel through their breakfast in order to get on with her main jobs for the day, which would be making mayonnaise for the prawn cocktails and whipping cream to put between the meringues. She also planned to make a chicken pie for Mr. Jones, in case he came home hungry in the middle of the night.

They were still at breakfast when the front doorbell rang.

"It is permitted that I again make an attempt to record your raven?" asked Professor Glibchick, for it was he. "Tomorrow I am returning to Freiherrburg, so this day is my last urgent opportunity."

"Oh, go ahead, suit yourself," grumbled Mrs. Jones, who was making the crust for Mr. Jones's chicken pie. "At least you kept Mortimer out from under my feet yesterday. Arabel, dearie, just run up to Mrs. Catchpenny, will you, and get me some more eggs and cream."

This time Arabel did not take Mortimer, who was enjoying himself sitting in front of Professor Glibchick and not saying a word, keeping his beak tight shut.

"*More* eggs and cream? My stars! Your Mum's making a real magnolious feast, isn't she?" said Mrs. Catchpenny. "You might let us have some of the leftovers! Has my Archibald caught that mouse for you yet?"

"As a matter of fact," said Arabel, "we haven't seen Archibald *or* the mouse today."

"Old moggie probably chased it out of doors somewhere," said Mrs. Catchpenny. "When it comes to catching mice, he's a real Turk; those people in Cantilever Green wouldn't have any problem if Archibald lived there."

"What happened in Cantilever Green?" asked Arabel.

"Why, it was in the paper, love; but I daresay your Ma's too busy cooking to read the news. Eaten out of house and home by mice, the people there have been; but now the mice have gobbled up all the food, it seems they've cleared out and gone somewhere else. Nobody knows where. But just let 'em show their whiskery noses here, my Archibald would soon have them sorted! They'd be glad enough to take themselves off to Parliament Hill or Wormwood Scrubs."

Arabel went home with the eggs and cream and this interesting news. But Mrs. Jones was having such a bothersome time with her blender that she said, "Don't worry me with that now, dearie; this mayonnaise has gone all hapsy-daisy. I don't know *what's* the matter with it. Put it in the freezer for me, will you?"

The way to make mayonnaise is by beating salad oil very slowly, a drop at a time, into whipped-up egg yolks. If you do it just right, it all turns into a thick, pale cream. But if you do it too fast or too slowly, it separates into yellow flakes and pale, oily juice. This was what had happened to Mrs. Jones, because she was using the blender she had bought from Happy-Pliances with a beater from the blender she had bought off a stall in Copernicus Road.

"It's gone all horrible," said poor Mrs. Jones. *"Everything's* going wrong for me today. My mayonnaise *never* did that before. Put it in the kitchen freezer and I'll give it another beating in twenty minutes, and perhaps it will come right then."

Arabel put the big, heavy glass bowl of oily stuff in the freezer compartment of the kitchen refrigerator. This had been switched to Extra Cold, to chill off Mr. Jones's chicken pie, in case he came home unexpectedly soon. Mr. Jones simply hated lukewarm food. "Let it be cold, or let it be hot," he often said. "I'll eat anything either way. But not in between. Cold food should be cold as ice, and hot should almost burn. For lukewarm food is never nice, and makes the stomach turn."

Mr. Jones often made up verses like this as he drove his taxi through the streets of London.

The freezer shelf where Arabel put the bowl of mayonnaise had become thickly coated with ice, which rose in a gentle slope to a little hill in the middle. When Arabel shut the freezer door, the glass bowl began to slide gently down this hill toward the door.

Mrs. Jones washed the plastic beater, reinserted it into the wrong blender, and poured a lot of cream into a bowl.

Professor Glibchick was attempting to encourage Mortimer by imitating other birdcalls.

"Tea—cher! Tea—cher!" he cried hopefully. "Be quick, be quick! Did he do it? Did he do it? I *do* like porridge. A little bit of bread and no cheese!"

"I'm ever so sorry but I'm afraid I can't give you any lunch," said Mrs. Jones, misunderstanding the professor. "Arabel and I weren't planning to have any ourselves." Distractedly she fitted a second beater into the blender. "If this cream doesn't whip soon I shall scream!"

Mortimer said nothing, but stared at the professor's tape recorder.

Mrs. Jones went on beating away at her bowlful of cream.

Mortimer was decidedly fond of cream. When he noticed what was going on, he began to shuffle along the kitchen counter in the direction of the bowl. Professor Glibchick moved slowly after him, holding out the microphone.

The cream was flying about like ocean spray in a storm at sea, because Mrs. Jones was using the wrong attachments on her blender. In fact there seemed to be more cream *outside* the bowl than there was in it. Drips of cream were everywhere—on the draining board, the wall, the windowpanes, Mrs. Jones's hair, which had gone snowy white, on her apron, Arabel's jersey, Professor Glibchick's microphone, and the geraniums on the windowsill. Soon Mortimer was covered with a thick layer of cream, so that he looked like an iced cake, made in the shape of a raven.

"Errrr!" he whispered softly, and edged even closer to the cream bowl. But still he did not speak.

Meanwhile the mice of Cantilever Green, resting in the disused railway shunting house at Vicarsbury Hill, were rudely woken by a party of students who had come to turn the building into a youth center. Doors flew open; buckets of disinfectant were sloshed about, brooms clattered, and dusters waved; the mice had to scramble out of the building at frantic speed. Because they were excellently organized they were able to do this without being discovered, but it was a terribly close thing. They all found a temporary refuge next door in a shabby old cinema—the Vicarsbury Electric Palace.

"We can't stay here long, though," said Scout F Stroke B7, who had gone ahead to check the building, "for the afternoon program starts at twelve noon and the doors open at eleven thirty. It's my belief, mates, that the best thing we can do now is to press on to Rumbury Town. The distance isn't far, and the weather is helpful."

The weather in London was foggy. A thick sea mist had drifted up the River Thames. It made people cough, and all those who could were staying indoors. Not many were about to notice the mice, as they scurried down gutters and across back gardens and along the tops of walls and over roofs and under gates and cars.

So far the migration from Cantilever Green had been highly successful. Not a mouse had been lost.

At about this time Mr. Jones was driving south down the highway with his friend Mr. MacDoritch. They were both in a very cheerful and festive mood. They had passed an exciting day watching the Highland Games, and Mr. MacDoritch's son Dougal had won his caber-tossing contest. But the weather in Scotland had turned very nasty, and the two friends were returning earlier than they had planned.

"Besides, I can't get on with that food they eat in Scotland," said Mr. MacDoritch. "All those collops, and that porridge, and the stuff they call Inky-Pinky—let alone Clapshot! I don't fancy it at all. Give me a good plate of bangers and mash any day!"

He took a swig from a bottle of GlenScrabble Cream Whisky, and added, "But I will say this—the drink's not so bad."

"My missis," said Mr. Jones, "always has a chicken pie waiting for me when I've been away. Prime, her chicken pies are: done with a little bit of ham, to give a relish to the gravy, and a touch of curry, and a hard-boiled egg sliced up in the middle." He smacked his lips, thinking of it.

"Care for a drop of GlenScrabble, Ben?" said Mr. MacDoritch, taking another himself.

"Not while I'm driving, David, thank you," said Mr. Jones. "I'll take one when we're back in Rainwater Crescent. Shouldn't be more than an hour now. I'll phone Martha from the next service area, just to let her know we're on our way." Then he remembered about the

Rumbury Ladies' Club. "Oh, blimey! All those old biddies are coming to our house tomorrow. Well, I'll just have to get up real early and go out; I'm not getting mixed up in that shebang—I'd sooner be dragged over Ben Nevis by my toenails."

"Still you're lucky to have a missis who's keen on cooking," said Mr. MacDoritch. "My old woman couldn't cook hot water for a barber."

"Martha's a great cook," said Mr. Jones. "And she keeps the house lovely—not a match end out of place."

Then the two men began planning a caber club they intended to start in Rumbury Town. They had both enjoyed watching the caber tossing at the Highland Games, and wished to introduce this sport in the south.

They had brought back some cabers with them, lashed to the roof of the cab. A caber is the trunk of a young pine tree with the branches roughly trimmed off.

At about this time Mrs. Jones, looking into her cream bowl, let out a piercing wail of despair.

"What's the matter, Ma?" asked Arabel, who was arranging the custard glasses. She had polished them and put a lettuce leaf in each one. Then she added a slice of cold potato to hold the lettuce in place. Next she would put in three or four prawns; or that was the idea.

Arabel and her mother had not yet been into the pantry and discovered that Archibald had eaten all the prawns.

"This cream!" wailed Mrs. Jones. "This cream has turned into *butter*! I swear there's a hoodoo on me. I never, never, in all my born days, had cream turn to butter. I didn't know such a thing could happen! Why didn't it whip? That's what I want to know!"

"Shall I put it in the freezer?" suggested Arabel. "Will that turn it back to cream?"

At this moment the telephone rang. Mrs. Jones went to answer it, wiping cream off her nose, her eyebrows, her hair, her apron, and her wedding ring.

"Martha?" said Mr. Jones's voice. "Just phoning to let you know that I'll be home in about an hour from now. The weather turned nasty. I'm at Towcester."

"Toaster," said Mrs. Jones. "That's where the mouse went. However did you know that, Ben?"

"Know what? Have you made me a chicken pie, Martha?"

"Yes I have; and oh, Ben, I shall be *ever* so pleased to see you. All my mixers have gone peculiar, and the cream's turned to *butter!*"

At this moment the phone beeped and the Joneses were cut off from each other.

"Your missis all right?" asked Mr. MacDoritch, noticing that Mr. Jones looked puzzled.

"She kept on about toast and butter. I couldn't make head nor tail of it."

"You'll know soon enough," said Mr. MacDoritch.

Arabel had picked up the bowl of cream-turned-to-butter and was walking toward the kitchen fridge. Mrs. Jones had just left the phone when it rang again, and she turned back to answer it. Arabel stopped to listen.

"Is that Mrs. Martha Jones?" said a lady's voice. "Oh, good, I'm so glad! Mrs. Jones, I'm just phoning to tell you that a slight mistake has been made. I am Mrs. Shanklin, Secretary of the Rumbury Ladies' Kitchen Club."

"Wh—what's that?" quavered Mrs. Jones, thinking with a wild hope that perhaps the Secretary was telephoning to say that the Club would not be coming to Number Six, Rainwater Crescent, tomorrow after all. "What was that you said, dear?"

"I made a silly mistake in the date, Mrs. Jones. Only in *your* letter, luckily! All the rest of the ladies in the club had it right. The *actual* date of the club meeting is August 27, that's today, Mrs. Jones. So the ladies will begin arriving at your house quite soon, in about half an hour from now. But they won't mind if they take you a little by surprise, all things considered, ha, ha! And anyway, I expect you are all ready for them, aren't you?" The Secretary chuckled again. "I know that most of our lady members, when their home is chosen, start getting ready days and days and *days* ahead of time!"

Mrs. Jones glanced frantically behind her, at Mortimer smothered with cream like a frost-covered statue, at Professor Glibchick with his tape recorder, at Arabel holding the bowl of butter, and lastly at something coming down the stairs that she simply failed to recognize.

In fact it was Archibald, with another layer of feathers on top of the first. He had woken feeling thirsty (after all the prawns) and decided that he needed some condensed milk.

"Yes. I see. Thank you for phoning, dear," croaked Mrs. Jones to the Club Secretary, and she put the phone receiver back on its rest. Then she had another look at Archibald, and still he didn't make any sense to her.

Then she tottered back to the kitchen, where a lot of things were just about to happen.

Mortimer had become interested in a blue knob on the blender which was standing on the kitchen counter. He sidled along to the blender and pressed the blue knob with his beak, quite hard. This violently released the mixing beaters, which flew across the kitchen and clattered against the door of the freezer. They fell on the floor, startling Arabel, who dropped the bowl of cream-turned-to-butter, and only just missing Senior Scout F Stroke B7, who had come on ahead of the Can-

tilever Green mice in order to make certain that everything in the promised land was still the way he had
reported it.

The back door had been open, so he had come in
that way.

At this moment also Archibald strolled in through the
door leading to the front hall.

Scout F Stroke B7 took one look at Archibald and
started back the way he had come. In fact he made it
from the refrigerator to the doormat in one-thirteenth
of a second, thus establishing a world record for the
fifty-one-centimeter dash, if anybody had been timing
him.

Archibald never noticed F Stroke B7. He was looking at all the cream scattered about the kitchen, and the butter on the floor. But what he wanted was condensed milk. He said, "Morow?" in his deep bass voice.

Meanwhile inside the freezer the bowl of separated mayonnaise, which had been sliding down a gentle ice slope for the last half hour, slid the last ten centimeters when the beaters thudded against the freezer door, burst open the door, and fell out, tipping half its contents onto the kitchen floor, and the other half onto Mr. Jones's chicken pie, which was cooling on the shelf below.

Mortimer, delighted and excited by this dramatic and unexpected result of his pressing the blue knob on the blender, turned and swallowed Professor Glibchick's tape recorder and microphone. He did it so quickly and neatly that the professor, for several minutes after, could not really believe what had happened; he kept staring about him in a perplexed manner, as if he expected that the lost appliance would turn up under the kitchen table or in the vegetable rack.

Since nobody offered Archibald a saucer of condensed milk, he moved in a leisurely way to the pantry door and expertly opened it.

Arabel, who had been gazing in stupefaction at

Archibald (at least she supposed it *must* be Archibald under all those feathers), leaped to shut the pantry door and shoo the cat away. But she looked into the pantry and gasped, "Ma! Someone's eaten all the prawns!"

"What?" said Mrs. Jones. She went to look too, and almost fainted. Then, getting a hold on herself, she said, "Well—the ladies will just have to have scones and butter and cakes and meringues and coffee in a jug. I'll put a kettle on. The ladies are coming *today*, Arabel—in about half an hour!"

"Oh, *Ma!*" said Arabel. She thought for a minute and said, "As the cream's turned to butter and is on the floor, we could stick the meringues together with marmalade."

"That's ever such a clever idea, Arabel, dearie," said her mother. "I'll run up and get the meringues, and you can be doing that."

She started upstairs.

At this time, most of the ladies of the Rumbury Town Kitchen Club were gathering not far off, at the end of Rainwater Crescent. Some had come on bikes, others had walked, some had alighted from buses, and others had been brought by their husbands or had driven themselves in cars. There were a great many of them. In fact there was something of a traffic jam at the end of the Crescent, since half the road was torn up because workmen were digging with pneumatic drills, looking for a leaking gas main. The pneumatic drills were making a lot of noise, but nothing like so much as the voices of the ladies of the Kitchen Club, who sounded like starlings at the end of the day when it is getting dark.

As a matter of fact it *was* getting dark. The fog had become thicker, so that the ladies (all dressed in their best) looked like guests at a ghosts' party. Some of them had bought newspapers at Mrs. Catchpenny's shop. Others had listened to radio or TV news; and they were all worriedly discussing the terrible wave of mice that had been seen flowing northward through London. A police helicopter had spotted the mice crossing Three Keys shunting yard at 7:30 a.m. and radioed the news back to headquarters. Now the mice were being tracked by radar and their course plotted out by police computers. And at this moment a police squad car came hooting along from the other end of Rainwater Crescent. The driver stopped and put out his head.

"Better get back to your homes, ladies! The mice are coming this way!"

"Oh my cats alive!" cried the members. "Should we climb Rumbury Church Tower? Or the multistory car park? Mercy, I can't stand mice! My hubby goes after them with a blow torch. Mine uses a staple gun. Mine sprays them with oven spray. Oh, save me! If I saw *one* mouse I should drop dead—let alone thirty thousand! Can't they turn them back? Whatever shall we do?"

Now a most bloodcurdling scream was heard coming from Number Six.

In fact it was Mrs. Jones, who had just discovered her ruined meringues.

"Aaaaaaa-ooooooh! *All my meringues!* Every last one

of them! It was that bird done it! Just wait till I get at him to wring his neck! Out of my house he goes, neck and crop, this instant minute!"

Mrs. Jones came down the stairs like a wild person, carrying a tray of flattened meringues with a lot of hairs sticking to them. Meanwhile Professor Glibchick was mourning, "My tape recorder! My tape! With my ouzel calls, my gaggle of geese, my dopping of shelldrake, my chattering of choughs, my scintillation of swans! That barbarous bird has eaten them, every one. Oh, why did I ever come to this atrocious country?"

Mrs. Jones seized a rolling pin, looking so furious that Professor Glibchick hastily made for the door; he thought she was angry because he had insulted her country. Anyway there was no sense in his staying now that he had no tape recorder.

Mortimer started walking after Professor Glibchick. He had a plan.

Arabel, who had been picking up bits of butter from the floor, exclaimed anxiously, "But Ma! Look, there's cat hairs all over those meringues. It wasn't Mortimer who squashed them—it must have been Archibald!"

While these things were happening, Mr. Jones and his passenger drew up at the other end of the Crescent (Mr. MacDoritch lived just around the corner in Rumbury Marsh Lane). By now the fog was so thick that they could hardly see the police squad car, or the workmen with their drills, or the ladies of the Kitchen Club.

"Home at last!" sighed Mr. Jones, stretching. "*Now* I

won't say no to a drop of GlenScrabble—and thank you kindly, Davie."

Mr. MacDoritch's wife was a member of the Club. Peering through the fog he recognized her, as she had very bright red hair.

"That you, Floss!" he called. "Got a crumpet for my breakfast? I've had enough of those baps, I can tell you! Look! I've brought home a caber, Floss! Just you wait till you see how I can toss it, Floss! Come on, Ben, let's give the girls a treat!"

But Mr. Jones was looking in amazement at the road, and saying, "My stars! I wouldn't have thought it could happen after one swig of that GlenScrabble; it must be rare powerful stuff. I'd be ready to swear I could see mice all over the road. Look at the ground!"

But Mr. MacDoritch was taking no notice of the ground. He pulled a caber off the cab luggage rack and hurled it like a javelin along Rainwater Crescent. It hit the elbow of one of the men operating pneumatic drills; the drill slipped and pierced a water main. A terrific jet of water shot up into the air, scattering the Kitchen Club ladies like leaves in a gale. In two seconds there wasn't a lady to be seen in the Crescent.

Meanwhile the mice, who had just arrived like a gray tide sweeping over the ground, were being addressed, at peril of his life, by dauntless Scout F Stroke B7, who had run up onto the top of a mailbox. He was shouting at the top of his voice: "Back! Back every one of you. Conditions here have seriously deteriorated! The people here have lethal flying beaters of every size, pressure hoses, and, worst of all, giant four-legged catbirds! Back, back to Vicarsbury! Assemble at the Electric Palace."

In fact, Archibald had not noticed F Stroke B7. He had licked some cream from the floor and walls and, as nobody would give him any condensed milk, he had contemptuously eaten a custard tart or two and gone back to sleep on his dust cloths.

The mice, horrified at F Stroke B7's words, turned and fled like a moving dark-gray carpet. They went in the opposite direction from the ladies; so the two parties never met.

" 'Struth!" said Mr. Jones, scratching his head. "Getting old, I must be. Spots before my eyes! I'll be glad of Martha's chicken pie and a bit of shut-eye."

He made for his home, but on the doorstep he encountered a blue-haired lady.

"Oh—are you Mr. Jones?" she said. "Perhaps you'd be kind enough to inform Mrs. Jones that today's Club Meeting has been cancelled, due to—due to unforeseen circumstances. I am Mrs. Shanklin, the Secretary." She gasped a little nervously as she saw Mortimer come out of the door; then ran to her car and drove away.

Mortimer looked after Professor Glibchick, who was trudging dispiritedly away up the Crescent, then opened his beak, puffed out his chest, and let out a terrifically loud shout. "NEVERMORE!!"

Professor Glibchick turned, shook his fist at Mortimer, then shrugged and went on his way.

"All right, all right, Mortimer, all right, old boy, no

need to take on so," said Mr. Jones, who thought Mortimer was welcoming him. Going inside, he called, "Martha, are you there? Got a chicken pie for me, have you? Managed all right without me, did you?"

Mrs. Jones dropped the rolling pin, with which she had been just about to give Archibald the surprise of his life. She ran into the front hall. Meanwhile Arabel quietly bundled Archibald into the garden. "I think you've stayed with us long enough," she said to Archibald. "Thank you for frightening the mouse. I expect you can find your own way home."

Archibald shrugged, and set off for the corner shop.

Mrs. Jones gave her husband a tremendous hug.

"Oh, Ben! *Am* I glad to see you! Oh, it *is* nice to have you back!"

"Here, steady on, Martha, what's the matter?" said Mr. Jones, looking in a puzzled way round his kitchen, which seemed to be splashed with cream all over the walls, and carpeted with butter and oily mayonnaise. "Been having a bit of trouble, then?" he said.

"Oh, it was nothing, really," said Mrs. Jones. She wiped her eyes and added, "But my little Polish mixer that you gave me has gone wrong. I'd be *ever* so glad if you could mend that, Ben; after you've had a rest and a bit of chicken pie."

The mice of Cantilever Green were never seen again in Rumbury Town. Indeed some of the ladies of the Kitchen Club declared that the whole thing was a false rumor; probably put about by the Jones family, so that they would not have to entertain the Club members. Nobody seems quite certain where the mice have gone; but the police think they may have settled in the Albert Hall.

Mortimer and Archibald the cat have remained fast friends. Archibald often strolls along to the garden of Number Six, where he licks Mortimer while Mortimer scratches his ears; then they play rather rough games. But Mrs. Jones won't allow Archibald in her house; she still remembers those prawns, and those trays of meringues.

Professor Glibchick was made happy because on his sea passage back to Freiherrburg he was able to record the call of a sea spink saying, "Pray, take a Mediterranean biscuit." But he still hopes to come back sometime and tape Mortimer saying "Nevermore."

ARABEL'S BIRTHDAY

2

There were visitors at Number Six, Rainwater Crescent
Mr. Jones's cousin Gladys Line had come up to London
to have a lot of special work done on her teeth at Rumbury Dental Hospital. This was going to take several days,
so she was staying in Rainwater Crescent for a week.
Her husband, Ray Line, who owned his own moving
company, had driven her down from Benwick-on-Tavey,
where the Lines lived, along with two huge suitcases full
of clothes, and their daughter Annie, who was just Arabel's age. Ray left his wife and daughter with the Joneses,
and then drove up north again with a load of brass fire
tongs, two mahogany tables, and a love seat.

Just because somebody is the same age as you does
not always mean that you are fond of them, and Arabel
was not very fond of her cousin Annie, who had platinum blond curls, and eyes the color of curried beans,
and a little squeaking whiny breathless voice in which
she was always saying things that had better not have
been said.

"Mummy, I saw Uncle Ben dip his finger in his soup
to see if it was hot—that's not very nice, is it? Ooh,

Mummy, Arabel put a HUGE spoonful of jam on her bread. Mummy, Aunt Martha's porridge isn't as good as yours, she doesn't put molasses and raisins in it. Mummy, Uncle Ben gave Arabel a much longer push on the swing than he did me, it's not *fair*. Mummy, Arabel's got slippers like rabbits and I haven't, it's not *fair*."

Many things happened to Annie that were not fair; or she thought they were not; other people had different opinions.

"Ask me, that child ought to have been parceled up at birth and posted off to Pernambuco," said Mr. Jones. He said this quietly to his wife in the garden, where he thought no one else could hear, but little Annie was sitting under the wheelbarrow, and she scrambled out and ran indoors to her mother, asking, "Mummy, Mummy, why does Uncle Ben say I ought to have been posted to Pernambuco, where is Pernambuco, Mummy?"

"Ooo werp oh oo arhing ee ey hing ush ow," said Annie's mother, who had just come back after a day spent at the dental hospital.

Annie had brought a great many of her own toys with her in the moving van, to prevent her becoming bored at Number Six, Rainwater Crescent, while Cousin Gladys was at the hospital having her teeth fixed. The things that Annie had brought were much more expensive and complicated than Arabel's toys: there was computer golf, and an electronic exercise bicycle, and some radio-controlled tiddlywinks, a centrally heated doll's house, a small infrared oven that really roasted, magnetic dominoes, a computer guitar that would make up its own

music and play without your needing to do anything, a
book that would read aloud when you opened it (but it
always read the same story, which was rather boring), a
skateboard that ran on solar energy, a chess set that
played games against itself, and lots of other things
besides.

A lot of these toys didn't seem to need humans at all.

Arabel thought they seemed as if they would prefer
to play by themselves, without being bothered to include
Annie and Arabel in what they were doing. And many
of them were so complicated—with their plugs and
cables and switches and instrument panels and control
boxes—that they needed Mr. Jones, first to start them

up, and then to stay around and keep an eye on them to make sure they didn't go wrong, heat up red hot, run out of fuel, chop somebody's arm off, or roll away, tossing out sparks, through the front door and into Rainwater Crescent. Mr. Jones soon became fed up with this. He became tired of Annie's voice squeaking, "Uncle Ben! Come *quick!* The doll's house is overheating again. The infrared oven's letting off its warning whistle. Uncle *Ben!*"

Mr. Jones said he had better things to do—such as driving his taxi—than sit all day keeping an eye on radio-controlled tiddlywinks. And, when the computer guitar had given Arabel quite a bad electric shock, Mr. Jones carted a whole lot of Annie's toys up to the attic and locked them away, despite her grumbles.

"They can't do any harm there," he said. "Besides, *I'm* not going to replace them if they get broken while the kid's here. Those things probably cost a fortune. Let her play with them when she's back home, and shock herself to death. Besides, if they're locked up, Mortimer can't get at them."

This was true, even Annie could see. Mortimer, the Jones family's raven, had, from the start, taken a huge amount of interest in Annie's toys; his black eyes sparkled bright as jet beads when first one glittering complicated object and then another was carried into the house by Cousin Ray Line.

Mortimer would dearly have liked to swallow the radioactive building bricks, and squeeze inside the centrally heated doll's house, and have a ride on the electronic bicycle, and look at his own bones through the X-ray box, and roast something in the infrared oven; he looked very downcast and sulky when Mr. Jones packed all these things in the attic, and locked the door, and slipped the key onto the ring that he always carried in his pocket.

"*Nevermore* . . ." muttered Mortimer to himself.

But he did not give up hope of getting into the attic. One day—when all the family were out . . .

One thing that Mr. Jones did not lock away, for she would not let him, was little Annie Line's Winky Doll, Mabel. Annie insisted on keeping Mabel by her wherever she went. This creature was larger than Annie and Arabel—*much* larger than Mortimer; it could walk, and nod its head, and wink its eye, and dance, and shake hands, and skate (that is, if you put it on ice and strapped skates onto its feet); and it could give a horrible smile, and put its finger to its lips, and whisper, *"Listen! I'll tell you a secret!"*

Then, if you leaned your ear close beside its mouth, it would whisper something into your ear.

Annie was always putting her ear beside the Winky Doll's mouth and listening to what it whispered. Then she would burst out into loud giggles and say, "Oooooh! Winky Doll's just told me EVER such an exciting secret, and I'm not going to tell it to YOO-OO!"

After a day or two of this, Arabel waited for a chance when her Cousin Annie was out in the garden, asking Mr. Jones for the twentieth time to stop his digging and give her a push in the swing.

"Ooh, Uncle Ben, please push me, please, Uncle Ben, please, Uncle Ben!"

While this was happening, Arabel put her ear close to the Winky Doll's mouth and pressed its whisper button. The Winky Doll winked like mad, and nodded its head ever so many times, but all that Arabel actually managed to hear was "Gabble-gabble-gabble-gabble, rhubarb-rhubarb-rhubarb."

This was quite disappointing.

Perhaps the Winky Doll won't whisper for me because I'm not its proper owner, Arabel thought.

Or perhaps it never does whisper a real secret.

Mortimer the raven had taken a strong dislike to the Winky Doll from the very start. He hated the knowing smile on its fat face, and he hated the way it winked its eye and nodded its head. He hated its clothes, which were checked cotton with a great many patches sewn on all over. He hated its blue rolling eyes and its fat pudgy hands, and worst of all he hated the way it whispered secrets to little Annie Line.

Mortimer could not stand being left out of anything.

If secrets were being whispered, he wanted them whispered to *him*.

"*Kaaaark,*" he grumbled furiously, each time Annie said, "Winky Doll's told me a secret and I'm not going to tell yoo-oo. . . ."

"Never mind, Mortimer," said Arabel, who quite sympathized with what Mortimer was feeling, "*I'll* tell *you* a secret," and she whispered to him, "Pa's making me a seesaw for my birthday."

But Mortimer was not appeased by this news. For one thing, he already knew about the seesaw, because he had watched Mr. Jones dig a deep hole, down at the far end of the garden, and sink a post in the hole, and set it in cement; and he had also spent some time in Mr. Jones's garden shed workshop, while the hinge was being fitted on the seat part of the seesaw; until Mr. Jones noticed that Mortimer had swallowed half a jarful of brass upholstery tacks, and requested him to leave.

The fifth day of Cousin Gladys's visit was Arabel's birthday. The seesaw had been finished, ready for use. As well as the seesaw, Arabel had been given, by her mother, a little marble pastry board and rolling pin, also a small pudding bowl, flour sifter, wooden spoon, and a cheesegrater, so that she could make pastry or cheese straws if she wanted to. Mortimer the raven was very fond of cheese straws. From her father Arabel had a set of gardening tools, spade, pitchfork, rake, hoe, watering can, and a wheelbarrow. Mortimer at once wanted to ride in the wheelbarrow, which was exactly the right size for him.

"I've bought you some tulip and daffodil bulbs too," said Mr. Jones. "Otherwise, as it's October, there wouldn't be much you could plant. But you can put the bulbs in now, and then you'll see them come up in the spring."

Arabel was very happy with her presents. She also had a toy dentist's set from Annie, a red handbag from Cousin Gladys, and, from Great-Uncle Arthur, a packet of six Mortimer bars.

Mortimer bars were a new kind of chocolate bar that had just been invented. They had layers of butterscotch, nuts, marzipan, and crumbly biscuit, wrapped in a thick chocolate coating.

Arabel liked them because of the butterscotch, nuts, and biscuit; Mortimer liked them because of the name. The name had nothing to do with Mortimer really; Fun-Folks Foods, Ltd., the chocolate company who made the bars, had never heard of Mortimer. They chose the name because it began with an M, for they already had several other chocolate bars with M names, Monarch and Macho and Monster and Magpie (which was black and white chocolate). Now there were big posters all over London, especially in Underground stations, showing a frantic mother and her little boy who was howling with hunger. The caption underneath the picture said:

> She should have
> bought him a
> MORTIMER!

Mortimer was delighted with these posters, and let out a loud *"Kaaaark"* of satisfaction whenever he saw his own name written up so large. (Mortimer was not able to read many words. But Arabel had taught him to recognize his own name when it was printed.)

Little Annie did not think highly of Arabel's presents. "Who wants a crummy old *cooking set?*" she said. "That's only for *babies*. And who wants to work in the *garden*? I'd sooner ride on my exercise bicycle. And as for those mingy chocolate bars . . . ! When it's *my* birthday, *my* Dad gives me a *huge* box of chocolates, five layers deep, that costs pounds and pounds and pounds, and I'm allowed to eat the chocolates till I'm sick."

"Fine goings-on, I must say," said Mrs. Jones.

"But with the Mortimer bars," pointed out Arabel, "you can win half a million pounds."

Arabel was right about this. Fun-Folks Foods, Ltd., had launched their new chocolate bar with an advertising campaign that told the public: "Save the wrappers from twenty different Mortimer bars, fit them together, and make yourself a map that will lead you to the exciting spot where a solid block of gold is buried worth £500,000! Five hundred thousand pounds!"

Every Mortimer bar had part of a map printed on the inside of its wrapper. When you had managed to collect the twenty different bits that made up the whole map, and stuck them all together in the right order, you had to solve the secret clues printed on the map, which told you where the gold was buried. It might be anywhere in the whole country. The map was dotted all over with little pictures of people and animals doing different things, and clues about these activities. "Emus bury wart," said one clue. "Subway, Mr. True?" said another. "We may rub rust," said another, and another said "A rum ruby stew."

Arabel and Mortimer had already collected more than twenty Mortimer bar wrappers. They had not actually eaten all that number of chocolate bars; but Mortimer was extremely sharp at spotting the gold-purple-and-brown wrappers on the pavement, or in trash cans, or on Rumbury Waste, where he and Arabel sometimes went roller skating.

Mrs. Jones did not approve of Mortimer picking up the wrappers.

"They're sure to be covered with germs," she said.

But Mortimer was very quick and clever at flipping them up with his beak and whipping them under his wing, and not bringing them out until he was back at home. He and Arabel had a wooden cigar box where they kept their collection of wrappers.

Some of the twenty wrappers that Arabel and Mortimer had saved were duplicates; they did not yet have a complete set of all that were needed. However, with Great-Uncle Arthur's six, there seemed a good chance that they might have the whole set.

"But you're not to go unwrapping and eating them all at once!" warned Mrs. Jones. "One a day—after dinner. You can cut each bar into three bits, one for each of you."

Mortimer's eyes sparkled at this, but Annie said, "That's not *fair*! That's *mean*! *My* Mum lets me eat a whole bar whenever I want to, *and* as many chocolates as I like."

"Yes, and look at your spotty face," said Mrs. Jones, but she said this to herself, not aloud, for she did not want to be unkind to a guest. Not that Annie took any pains to be kind to the Jones family. She pinched Arabel to make her get off the swing, poked Mortimer with her doll's parasol, told Mr. Jones that his face was too red, and grumbled because Mrs. Jones did not have ice cream at every meal.

Arabel's birthday, a Saturday, was fine and sunny, so

she went into the garden directly after breakfast to plant her new bulbs with her new gardening tools. Annie didn't want to be left out of this, although she despised gardening, so Arabel let her have half the bulbs, and take turns with the spade, trowel, and rake, which were red, with yellow handles.

Mortimer preferred to dig holes with his beak.

"Perhaps we'll find the gold Mortimer bar, if we dig enough holes," said Annie. "It might be in this garden as well as anywhere," and she began digging holes all over Mr. Jones's garden beds, until he came out of his work shed and stopped her.

When they had planted all the bulbs (Annie planted hers upside down, because she said that way they would grow downward and come up in Australia; Arabel was not very happy about this), they played on the new seesaw.

Annie and Arabel were just about the same height and weight; they found they could use the seesaw very well together.

Mortimer did not like being left out. He jumped up and down with annoyance, and shouted *"Nevermore!"* so many times that neighbors in gardens on each side began to complain.

"That bird is a pest," they said. "There's never any peace while he's around."

"He wants a turn on the seesaw," said Arabel.

"Well, give him one, for mercy's sake!" said Mr. Cross next door.

"He can't have *my* place," said Annie.

"Come on, Mortimer, you can sit on my end," said Arabel, and she got off and lifted Mortimer onto her seat. Mr. Jones had set in crossbars for a handhold; Mortimer clutched the crossbar with his claw.

Unfortunately he was far too heavy for Annie on the seesaw; Mortimer had recently swallowed an iron wedge, a claw hammer, and an old metal doorstop, in Mr. Jones's workroom; and when he sat on the seesaw, the other end, with Annie on it, shot up into the air and stayed there.

"Oooooh! I'm slipping! Let me down!" shrieked Annie, high up on her end of the seesaw.

Mortimer flopped off his end, and Annie came down with a bump.

"What a shame," said Arabel. "Let's try with both of us on one seat and Mortimer on the other."

But even so, he was too heavy for them.

"You've been eating too much, you fat old pig of a rook!" said Annie rudely. "Come on, Arabel, let's play dressing up."

Mortimer was offended, and also disappointed because he had been looking forward to a turn on the seesaw. He ruffled out all his feathers, went into a sulk, and walked away to watch Mr. Jones, who was burning up dead cabbage stalks and thorn twigs in the garden incinerator, along with the chips of wood left over from the seesaw.

Mortimer watched Mr. Jones with great attention. Then he began bringing things to be burned; first he fetched some sticks, but Mr. Jones said they were his pea sticks and were being saved for next year; next Mortimer found the cardboard box that had had the bulbs in it, which Mr. Jones let him burn; then he brought the paper wrappings from Arabel's tool set, and a whole tangle of garden raffia that had rotted, so Mr. Jones let him burn those things too.

"Now that's enough, Mortimer," said Mr. Jones at this point. "I've got other things to do than watch a raven burning rubbish. You run along and play with the girls."

Mr. Jones went off to drive his taxi.

Mortimer never ran anywhere. He walked away slowly, with his head sunk in his neck feathers.

The girls were in Arabel's room, dressing up in each other's clothes. Little Annie had brought from home an enormous suitcase full of dresses and pinafores and skirts and sweaters and jeans and shirts, all clean and new; she could have changed everything she had on, from the skin up, five times a day and still have had some things left over by the end of the visit. So Arabel was having quite an exciting time trying on her cousin's wardrobe. Unluckily Arabel herself did not have nearly so many clothes, and also she was thinner and a little shorter than Annie; Mrs. Jones had made her a new blue dress for her birthday but when Annie tried it on, she tore it at the neck.

"Your clothes are boring," said Annie. "Let's dress up in Auntie Martha's clothes and play Kings and Queens."

Without asking permission, Annie got Mrs. Jones's fur coat out of the black plastic mothproof clothes bag where it lived and put it on; then she made herself a crown from an empty ice-cream container cut into spikes.

When Mortimer discovered what the girls were doing, he was not interested. He had not the least wish to play Kings and Queens. He tried to get into the black plastic bag where Mrs. Jones's fur coat had been kept, which he had always wanted to do, but Arabel would not let him. So, while Arabel was making herself a crown out of three egg boxes stuck together, Mortimer went grumpily downstairs again. On the way up he had noticed the Winky Doll arranged in an armchair in the living room, staring at the blank television screen. (Annie had left the TV switched on for the Winky Doll, but Mrs. Jones had switched it off, muttering, "Dolls watching TV, what next?" before going back to her kitchen work.)

Mrs. Jones was busy making Arabel's birthday cake.

Mortimer went into the living room and tried to pick up the Winky Doll. But, although he was very strong, the doll was too floppy and bulky and awkward for him to carry.

"*Nevermore!*" he croaked to himself.

The Winky Doll's hands and feet were too fat and shiny for Mortimer's beak or claws to grasp them. At length he managed to drag the doll off the chair and onto the floor by its skirt; then he began hauling it across the floor by its hair. Some hair came out. And Mortimer knocked over a small table and a floor lamp.

At the sound of the table falling, Mrs. Jones called, "Arabel and Annie, what are you doing?"

"We aren't doing *anything*, Auntie Martha," called Annie from upstairs. Mrs. Jones went to see what this meant. She was very annoyed at finding Annie in her fur coat.

"*That* goes *straight* back in its satchel, and don't let me see you touch it again," she said. "And you'd better tidy up all this mess. What Cousin Gladys will say when she sees all Annie's nice new things crumpled up like that, I *do* not know."

"Oo werp oh oo arhing ee ey hing ush ow," was all that Gladys Line actually said when she came back from the dental hospital, but by that time, of course, the clothes had been folded up and put back in Annie's drawer.

Mrs. Jones was even more annoyed when she found that Arabel's new blue dress had been torn at the neck.

"You girls go and play *outside*," said Mrs. Jones, and she went back, with her lips pressed tight together, to the kitchen, to see how Arabel's birthday cake was getting on. The girls played radio-controlled tiddlywinks on the back doorstep.

While Mrs. Jones was upstairs, Mortimer had managed to drag the Winky Doll through the kitchen, out the back door, and down the sloping cement path to the garden incinerator behind the laurel bush. He propped the doll against the side of the incinerator and rested for a moment or two; all that dragging had been hard work. Then he flapped himself up and perched on the rim of the incinerator. Then he leaned down and took a good hold of the doll's hair with his beak.

Then, with one terrific jerk, twitch, flap, hoist, and scramble, he wrenched up the Winky Doll, hauled it over the rim of the incinerator, and dropped it down inside.

There were still some glowing ends of twigs and slivers of wood smoldering away under the ashes at the

bottom of the pile of burned garden rubbish. When the Winky Doll had stood on its head in the ashes for a few minutes, the dry blond hair began to burn; then, with a little spurt of flame, the frilly collar caught fire.

"Kaaaark!" said Mortimer, delighted; and he flopped

off the rim of the incinerator (which was rather too close
to the flames for comfort) and watched from the handle
of Mr. Jones's wheelbarrow, as, with a fluttering roaring
sound, the Winky Doll burned up completely. A thick
black column of smoke rose up from the foam rubber
with which the doll was stuffed. Quite soon there was
nothing left in the bottom of the incinerator but a squirmy
coil of shiny greasy black brittle stuff.

"Nevermore!" said Mortimer with deep satisfaction,
and he went away to sit on the bottom end of the seesaw,
and think about Mortimer bars, and milk chocolate, and
mince pies, and mushrooms, and all the other things he
liked to eat.

"Girls," said Mrs. Jones presently, seeing them on the
back step, "it'll be teatime soon. Why don't you take a
bit of exercise before tea, instead of just sitting there?"

Arabel and Annie stood up. If Arabel had been
on her own, she would have found plenty to do in
the garden: sweeping up leaves, picking bunches of
Michaelmas daisies to put in meat-paste jars, collecting
empty snail shells, and looking for nuts in the hazel
hedge behind Mr. Jones's work shed. But Annie did
not want to do any of those things; she said they were
boring.

"Let's get out the garden hose and water your bulbs
that we planted," Annie said.

"Pa doesn't like me to get out the hose," Arabel said
doubtfully.

"Well, he's not here," said Annie, and she dragged

out the hose, which was long and green and shiny, and lived in the shed, wound up on a kind of wheel.

Annie unwound a whole lot of the hose. Then she fitted the end of it over the garden tap and turned the tap on.

Annie had left the nozzle of the hose pointing toward Arabel, who was walking slowly toward Mortimer, still sitting on the seesaw; when Annie turned the tap full on, a sharp jet of water burst out of the hose nozzle and drenched Arabel from head to foot.

"Eeeech!" cried Arabel, in surprise; and Mortimer, who had climbed off the seesaw and started walking toward her, stopped short and gazed in astonishment. Next minute he got soused as well, for Annie, almost doubled up with laughter, grabbed the nozzle and turned it in Mortimer's direction.

Mortimer did not in the least mind being sprayed with water; his coat of black feathers was so thick and waterproof that most of the spray just ran off onto the grass. But he was very anxious to get a closer look at the hose; this was because, whenever Mr. Jones used it for watering the garden, he forbade Mortimer to come anywhere near, and, indeed, generally shut the raven inside the house while watering was being done. "For you know what would happen," he said. "That black monster would eat up the hose like spaghetti before you could say Columbus!"

So Mortimer had never been able to get a close look at the hose, and now he was not going to waste his

chance. He thought the hose looked as if it might be
made of licorice.

Just then Mrs. Jones came out with a couple of tea
cloths to hang on the line.

"Girls!" she called. "It's just going to be teatime. Birthday cake! Where are you?"

Then she saw Arabel, soaked from head to foot, with

her fair hair hanging plastered all around her like a yellow shawl, and the water streaming off her wet dress.

"*Arabel Jones!* What*ever* have you been *doing*?"

"Look out, Auntie Martha!" squeaked Annie in fits of giggles. "Or I'll turn the hose on you too!"

But at that moment Mortimer, who had been observing the length of shiny green hose very attentively, walked along it toward Annie, giving it, as he went, a series of brisk sharp stabs with his beak—just the way a cook cuts with a knife around the rim of a pastry tart—peck, peck, peck, peck, peck! At each peck along the pipe, out shot a jet of water. And the last one hit little Annie Line, and drenched her as thoroughly as her cousin.

Mrs. Jones, lips jammed together to stop her saying something she might later regret, went and turned off the garden tap. Then she jerked the lever that coiled the hose, and rewound it onto its wheel. Then she locked up the hose in the garden shed and pocketed the key.

"Just you wait till your father hears about this!" she said to Arabel. "Go along—indoors, the pair of you, and get out of those wet things."

"Shan't you let us have Arabel's birthday cake now?" pertly asked Annie Line, turning to stare at Mrs. Jones with her curried-bean eyes, as she slowly dripped her way upstairs, all over Mrs. Jones's pale-green stair carpet.

Annie was used to being in disgrace, which was a daily event with her at home; disgrace never lasted long in her family.

"We'll see," said Mrs. Jones grimly, following Arabel into the bathroom with a towel.

However, when Mr. Jones came home, which he soon did, for he had promised to be back in time for Arabel's birthday tea, he said, after hearing the story, "Well, Martha, it wasn't Arabel's fault—for it was Annie's idea to play with the hose. So I don't see why Arabel shouldn't have her birthday cake. And as for Mortimer, it's no more than you'd expect of *him.*"

"It's all that perishing little Annie—I could wring her neck," muttered Mrs. Jones. "Nothing but trouble since she's been in the house. Normally our Arabel's good as gold—and Mortimer at least is just himself, that's all you can say of him."

"Well, Annie's a visitor, you can't punish the child," said Ben, "and thank goodness she and Gladys are going on Monday; nothing too bad can happen between now and then," he added hopefully. "Let's go on and have the birthday tea, Martha."

So they had the birthday tea, in the kitchen, with a pink tablecloth over the big kitchen table, and candles on the pink cake, and Annie and Arabel rather clean and quiet, and Mortimer decidedly overexcited, swallowing the crackers as fast as they were pulled, sometimes even before they were pulled, as well as all the things that came out of them, riddles and whistles and rings and paper caps and plastic flowers.

Cousin Gladys returned from her day's treatment at the hospital and swallowed a cup of tea, but was unable to eat anything because of her teeth.

"Ooo werp oh oo arhing ee ey hing ush ow," she said. "Ahhy irhy, Arel eerie."

Later it was bedtime for the girls, and Annie began looking for her Winky Doll.

"That's funny, I thought I left her in the living room," she said. "I thought I left her in the armchair watching *Racing at Windsor.*"

"So you did, but I came in and switched off the program. Wasting television on dolls, indeed!" said Mrs. Jones.

"Did you put my Winky Doll away somewhere, Aunt Martha?"

"Didn't touch the object," said Mrs. Jones.

"Somebody knocked over the table and the light, and broke the bulb," said Mr. Jones, taking the broken bulb out of the floor lamp. "Was that you girls?"

They shook their heads.

Then Arabel noticed a button from the Winky Doll's dress lying on the carpet near the door. Just one button. And a tuft of hair.

A sudden awful thought came into her head.

"Mortimer," she said. "Did you take Annie's Winky Doll anywhere?"

"*Kaaark,*" said Mortimer dreamily.

"Mortimer. Where did you take the Winky Doll?"

Without the least hesitation, Mortimer proudly led the way to the garden incinerator. By now it was dark; they had to switch on the light outside the back door, and carry flashlights with them to shine on what Mortimer had to show them—which was a pile of ash. There was one brass button left among the ashes, and a blue eye.

"MORTIMER!!!"

Little Annie Line went into whooping hysterics, and had to be given hot milk with sherry and molasses in it.

"My Winky Doll!" she wept and hiccuped. "My Winky Doll! She knew all those secrets—and—and now she'll never tell them to me anymore!"

"Not a bad thing that, if you ask me," muttered Mr. Jones to himself. But to Cousin Gladys he said, "Of course we'll replace the blas—the doll, Gladys—as it was our raven that did the damage."

"She was the only one who told me secrets!" wailed Annie.

"Ah oo, Ben," said Gladys Line.

"I don't want any other doll!" screamed Annie. "I want my Whispering Winky! Just let me get at that Mortimer! I'll roast him in my infrared oven!"

"Kaaark," said Mortimer.

"I'll bathe him in a bowl of bleach and turn him white!"

"Kaaark."

"I'll stand him on his head in the blender and liquidize him."

"Kaaark."

"I'll stick him in the deep freeze and turn him into a block of frozen raven."

"Kaaark. Kaaark."

"I'll chop him into drumsticks with Dad's electric carving knife—"

"Ow, Annie! Oo erp oh oo arhing ee ey hing ush, ow," said her mother.

"*I* believe that child's got a temperature," said Mrs. Jones. "She'd better take a couple of Easydorm tablets, and stay in bed tomorrow."

To her husband later Mrs. Jones said, "All those wicked things she was saying she'd like to do to our Mortimer, the spoiled little madam! Why, I'm half scared of what she might try, if she had a chance to get at him. I'll keep her in bed tomorrow, out of harm's way, while Gladys has her last treatment."

"Just the same, I'd back Mortimer, if it came to it," said Mr. Jones. "I reckon he can take care of himself."

"I dunno, Ben. The look in that child's eye! She really had me scared."

Next day the travel plans of Gladys and Annie were upset by a telephone call from Annie's teenage brother Dick, to say that Ray Line had been involved in a highway pileup, and was in Benwick Hospital with a broken collarbone, and his van, full of plastic draining boards, was a write-off.

"Poor Gladys is *ever* so upset," said Mrs. Jones, telling her husband about this when he came home from taxi driving. "Now she's got to go home by train, and she says she doesn't know if she can face the journey, on her own, with Annie and all that luggage they brought. So I said I'd go to Benwick with her, and stay till Ray comes out of the hospital—though it'll mean taking Arabel as well. I thought I'd leave Mortimer with you, Ben."

"No. No. No!" said Mr. Jones. "Can't have that bird on his own in the house whenever I go out on a job, or around the corner for a pint. He'll have to travel along with you."

"Oh, Ben! I'd never manage all that *and* Mortimer."

"Then I'll have to come along on the train," said Mr. Jones. "See you to Benwick, put you all in a cab, then get the next train back to London. Can't use my taxi, the clutch wants fixing. It'd never get us to Newcastle."

"Oh, Ben! *Could* you? That's ever so thoughtful of you."

Cousin Gladys thought so too. "Ah oo, Ben—ah eyer oh ay och oo!"

But difficulties arose, and this plan almost got nipped in the bud, when Cousin Gladys and little Annie began seriously getting down to their packing. For everybody except little Annie had forgotten about the things in the loft—the exercise bicycle, the computer golf, the mechanized Ping-Pong, toy infrared oven, do-it-yourself X-ray kit, rubber dinghy, and a huge box of fireworks that Cousin Gladys had bought on her way back from the hospital one day because it would be Guy Fawkes Day soon.

"Can't take all *that* load," said Mr. Jones firmly. "We'd need a spare caboose all to ourselves. No—those things'll have to stay here till Ray gets his collarbone mended and his van replaced and comes to fetch them."

Since he was being so kind about traveling to Benwick with her, Cousin Gladys could not object to this, but little Annie was highly indignant.

"Leave all my lovely toys behind for that horrible bird to burn up? Not likely!"

"Oh, Annie! Ooo werp oh oo arhing eee ey hing!"

Annie stuck out her lip and scowled horribly. But Mr. Jones gave her such a quelling look that she turned quite pale and muttered, "Well, we *got* to take the fireworks. There wouldn't be any *point* to the fireworks, if we didn't have them for Guy Fawkes."

Finally the luggage was all packed and collected together—Arabel and Mrs. Jones's moderate-sized bags, to last them for a few days at Benwick, and Mrs. Jones's fur coat in its black plastic bag—"What d'you want to take your fur coat for, Martha?" demanded Mr. Jones. "You won't be doing anything posh in Benwick."

"It'll be cold up north, Ben. Besides, burglars might come here, while we're away, and steal it."

"Well, why not wear it then, instead of carrying it in that bag?"

"Wear my *fur coat* on the *train*? Are you crazy, Ben Jones?"

Then there was a huge pork pie in a plastic container inside a knapsack, which Mrs. Jones had made so no one would have to cook when they got to Cousin Gladys's house. And there was another knapsack with a picnic in it, to eat on the four-hour train journey. And there was Mortimer in his travel basket lined with an old pink blanket that had been Arabel's crib cover when she was smaller. There were Annie's and Gladys's enormous cases of clothes and the box of fireworks, which Annie had insisted on taking—besides another bag containing her radio-controlled tiddlywinks, magnetic dominoes, self-play chess set, and solar-powered skateboard. All these things were jumbled together at the foot of the stairs.

"Blimy," muttered Mr. Jones. "We don't need a taxi to take us to King's Cross—we need the Royal Coach."

Mr. Jones's friend Sid Ivy was driving them to the station.

Just as they had half the luggage out on the pavement, a police squad car pulled up alongside.

"You going away, Ben?" called Sergeant Pike, who was a friend of the Jones family.

"Martha and the kid are," said Mr. Jones. "I'll be back tonight. Why?"

"Oh, if you're coming back, that's OK. We're keeping a sharp eye on all unoccupied property around here just now. The Rumbury Rakes are out of jail, and they've had to shift out of the Palindrome because it's being pulled down."

"What's the Palindrome?" Annie asked.

"It's the old empty cinema opposite Rumbury Market."

"Who are the Rumbury Rakes?"

"The Rumbury Rakes are a gang of very dangerous criminals, young lady," said Sergeant Pike. "You'd better be thankful you don't have anything to do with them."

"Oh, Ben!" said Mrs. Jones fearfully. "Are you sure it's all right to go off and leave our house empty?"

"Don't be soft, Martha, of course it is. Sergeant Pike here will keep an eye on it, won't you, Jim?" said Mr. Jones impatiently. "Come on, come on, at this rate we'll miss the ten-thirty and maybe young Dick'll be there on the platform at Benwick wondering where we've got to. Hurry up, you kids, get some of that stuff loaded into the cab."

Everybody began dashing to and fro across the pavement, bumping into other people, tripping over things that other people had just put down, getting in each other's way, asking questions of everybody else and telling them what not to do.

"Where's the pork pie? Gladys, did you put in the toys?"

"Arabel! What have you done with the picnic?"

"Ben! You can't put those fireworks on top of my fur coat! Suppose they were to go off!"

From all the hurrying and scurrying, and the amount of luggage that was being shifted, anyone watching might have thought that the Jones family were leaving for a six-month trip to the Seychelles. At last they were all jammed in the cab, the two mothers on the backseat, with Annie between them, Arabel and Mr. Jones on the tip-up seats traveling backward. Annie was in a sulk because *she* wanted to be on a tip-up seat. Arabel was worried because Mortimer's travel basket was in the trunk instead of on her lap. That was because Annie had flatly refused to travel in a car with the raven.

"If I have to be as close to him as that, I'll scream and scream till I'm sick. I *hate* that bird!"

"She'll *have* to go with him in the train," said Mr. Jones grimly.

But his wife whispered to him, "Hush! Gladys gave Annie one of my Easydorm tablets in her breakfast cereal. She'll soon quiet down, go to sleep most likely. And *I* gave a tablet to Mortimer in one of my ginger-and-marmalade tarts. I reckon he'll sleep all the way to Benwick."

"That was smart of you, Martha," said Mr. Jones, who knew how partial Mortimer was to ginger-and-marmalade tarts. "Maybe, after all, we'll have a bit of peace and quiet on the trip."

What they didn't know was that Annie had snatched Mortimer's marmalade tart while he was looking hopefully at Mrs. Jones's black fur coat bag as it sat on the bottom step of the stairs.

Somehow they all managed to get themselves unloaded from the taxi at King's Cross, and onto the non-stop InterCity train to Benwick-on-Tavey.

Mr. Jones piled all the luggage into the racks—including Mortimer's raven basket. He failed to notice that the basket did not seem quite so heavy as it should have been.

"Will Mortimer be all right up there in the rack, Pa?" Arabel asked anxiously.

"He'll soon let us know if he's not," said her father. "You can rely on Mortimer for that."

Arabel nodded. She knew this was true. Mortimer would soon begin to shout and carry on if he wasn't happy. In any case he knew how to undo the lid of his basket.

After Arabel had looked out of the window for a while, at the flat country north of King's Cross, she took out the drawing book she had brought with her, and the old cigar box full of Mortimer bar wrappers, and settled down to working out how they should be fitted together. They were on the kind of train that had tables between the seats, so Arabel could do this job comfortably on the table.

Annie grumbled terribly at first, because Mr. Jones had not bought her a comic book, because her magnetic dominoes were at the bottom of a case full of clothes and she was not allowed to unpack it, because the buffet car was not open yet and she and Arabel could not go and buy packets of crisps and cans of Thirst-Aid; but then, just as Mr. Jones was muttering that he knew what *he'd* do with a young 'un that went on so, she fell into a deep sleep that lasted till past Newcastle and the end of the picnic lunch.

Meanwhile Arabel, all excited after several hours of hard thinking, cried out, "Pa! *Pa!* I believe I've put this together right! Look! It all fits! And, look, all these clues— 'A rum ruby stew,' and 'Wary Emu burst,' and 'Subway, Mr. True?'—if you move the letters about into a different order, they all spell the same thing!"

"And what's that?" asked Mr. Jones, yawning, for he had eaten two thick ham sandwiches and a large heavy piece of coconut cake. "Ask *me*, all these competitions do is get you to pay out more money."

"No, no, Pa, if you win this one you dig up a gold bar that's worth five hundred thousand pounds! And it's all because Mortimer has worked so hard collecting wrappers—I ought to get him down and tell him—"

"No, no, he's asleep, thank goodness, leave him be. So what do the clues spell then?"

"They all spell RUMBURY WASTE! And I believe that's where the gold bar's buried!"

"Eh? What?" said Mr. Jones, suddenly alert after all, and he took the maps all made out of Mortimer bar wrappers, which Arabel had carefully stuck together. It was a copy of a regular Ordnance Survey map, but the place names had been blanked out so there were just

paths and brooks and hills and copses and pylons and parish boundaries marked, and a bit of red road running along one side.

"Sure, that's Rumbury Waste," said Mr. Jones, after carefully studying the map. "I drive past it forty times a week, I ought to know. There's the water tower. There's the sewage plant. There's the Public Conveniences, there's the allotments. What gave you the idea, Arabel, lovey? My word, I believe you've gone and won us all that money! What do we have to do?"

"Phone that telephone number at the top of the map," said Arabel, all excited. "Give your name and the answer. And they'll give you the last clue, where to dig.

You'd better do it from Benwick Station, Pa, as soon as we get there, in case someone else has thought of the answer too."

Arabel's voice was joyful. If we win that money, she was thinking, it will pay for a horrible new Winky Doll for Annie, and a new hose for Pa; it isn't fair that he should have to pay for those things.

By now the train was running alongside the River Tavey, about to enter Benwick.

"Ay uh, Annie," said her mother.

Annie, who had fallen asleep again after lunch, yawned and stretched and grumbled. "We never had any *tea*. I wanted to have tea in the buffet car."

Everyone began standing up, and bumping into everybody else, putting books and magazines and knitting and candy wrappers into bags and cases. The train sighed to a stop and the automatic doors opened.

"Oh look—there's Auntie Clotilda!" yelled Annie joyfully. "And Uncle Swen! Perhaps they'll take us out to tea at Scotswood's!"

She jumped out of the train shouting, "Auntie Clotilda, Arabel's horrible old raven burned my Winky Doll! Wasn't he horrible?"

"Burned up your dolly? Oh, you poor little love," cried Auntie Clotilda, who was big and round and pink with yellow hair, and looked like the sort of thing you win at a fair by shooting six glass bottles with an air gun. Uncle Swen was small and fat and red-faced with glasses, and he put in a "Huff!" before everything he said, in order to make sure that everybody was listening.

"Uncle Swen will buy you another dolly, you poor little mite, won't you, Swen?" said Auntie Clotilda. "We've come to stay with your Mum till she's better."

"Huff! Buy the girlie another doll if she wants it," said Uncle Swen. "Mind you—huff!—never thought she cared for it all that much; never took any notice of it that *I* ever saw."

"Oh, sweetheart, of course she did—she loved every hair on its head—pleased to meet you dear, I'm sure," said Auntie Clotilda, who had not met Mrs. Jones before, and then she and Uncle Swen began bustling about, helping to get all the luggage out of the train, while Mr. Jones, seeing there was plenty of assistance, bolted away to find a telephone and ring up Fun-Folks Foods. Annie's brother Dick was there on the platform too; he had platinum hair like his sister, all curls, and a lot of teeth that stuck out, and red sunglasses, so that he looked like a white rat wearing a corduroy jacket. He gave Arabel a superior glance, but did not speak to her. Having taken all the luggage out, he and Uncle Swen began shifting it across the platform toward the exit. "What a lot of stuff," said Uncle Swen. "Anyone 'ud think you'd been away for a year, Gladys."

Arabel, who had been rather silent and shy at meeting all these new people, suddenly said, "Oh, careful, please! That's my raven—in the wicker basket."

"What?" said Auntie Clotilda with a screech. "You brought that *raven*? The one that ate Annie's Winky Doll? I'm not having that thing under the same roof

with me. Our poor little Peekaboo would have a heart attack at the sight of the nasty bird!"

"Huff! Quite agree!" said Uncle Swen. "Dangerous, nasty things. Give you citykosis as soon as look at you."

"He didn't eat the Winky Doll, Aunt Clotilda, he burned it up," said Arabel politely.

"Well, I'm sure!" said Mrs. Jones, quite affronted—
in spite of the fact that, when at home, she had plenty
of hard things to say about Mortimer. "I'm sure *we've*
no wish to push ourselves in where our raven's not welcome! Seeing as how you have got your brother and
sister-in-law to look after you, Gladys, Arabel and I may
as well travel straight back to London with Ben—"

"Huff! Best put the bird in the luggage locker till it's
time for your train back," said Uncle Swen.

"Oh, please no!" cried Arabel in horror; she was sure
that Mortimer would hate to wake up from his nap
and find that his travel basket was packed inside a left-
luggage locker.

"Oo'll ay aha uhuh o ee ehore oo oh, Arha?" said
Gladys, rather unhappy at the way the Jones family were
being treated.

Mrs. Jones glanced at the station clock and murmured
to Arabel, "It'll only be for an hour or so, lovey. Dad
was going to get the four o'clock back—" and while she
was still speaking, Annie and Dick had grabbed various
bits of the Joneses' luggage and raced off, giggling, toward the luggage lockers, which were in a big silvery
bank along one wall of the station. "Mind my fur coat—
it's in the black bag—" Mrs. Jones called after them
anxiously. "Mind the picnic basket, it's got breakables
in it!"

"Mind Mortimer!" called Arabel, even more anxiously.
She started to run after them. Uncle Swen and Aunt
Clotilda had bundled Cousin Gladys into a plum-colored

Ford Festina, calling, "You others come in a cab. We'll have a cup of tea waiting for you!" and they drove away.

At that moment Mr. Jones reappeared, looking white and wild-eyed.

"What is it, Pa, what's the matter?" cried Arabel. She stopped chasing Dick and Annie. "Couldn't you get through to Fun-Folks Foods?"

"Get through?" said Mr. Jones. "Get through? Oh yes, I got *through* all right."

Absently he took the key of the left-luggage locker that Dick Line handed him—it had a thick red round plastic disk on it, the size of a marshmallow, with a number. Mr. Jones put the key in his pocket.

"Ben? What *is* it?" wailed Mrs. Jones fearfully. "What's the matter? Why do you look so all-overish?"

"I got through to Fun-Folks Foods," said Mr. Jones, "and they told me—"

"Oh, Pa," cried Arabel, guessing, "has somebody else already—"

"Yes, they have! And who do you think phoned in with the right answer?"

"I can't guess, Pa. Somebody we know? Somebody nice?"

"It's that pack of hoodlums that call themselves the Rumbury Rakes," said Mr. Jones. "The man at Fun-Folks Foods told me that. He said I was the second person to come up with the correct solution. Fork O'Farrell, the leader of the Rumbury Rakes, phoned in at half-past seven this morning, and they were out on

Rumbury Waste, digging up the gold bar, at eight."

"Oh, Pa! What a shame!"

If Annie hadn't been staying with us, thought Arabel, I'd have had more time to work on that puzzle. I'd have finished it days ago.

But Mr. Jones hadn't finished.

"And where do you think the gang are *now*?" he said to his wife.

"Oh, Ben! They're not at *our*—"

"That's right! The cops spotted them on Rumbury Waste and chased them in a squad car—they're wanted for smuggling—and now they're holed up in Number Six, Rainwater Crescent. Is there a train back before the four o'clock?" he asked Dick Line. "If so, I'm taking it."

"Oh, *Ben*! You mean that pack of young monsters is in *our* home, using *our* soap and towels and eating my Fruity Crumble Cake?"

"They're eating it if they've got time," growled Mr. Jones. "Half the cops in North London are sitting around the house, the Fun-Folks Foods fellow told me, with smoke jets and pepper guns and sneezing-powder sprays—"

"Oh! My clean slipcovers!" wailed Mrs. Jones. "And the new bathroom linoleum, and twenty pounds you just spent on having the back door glass mended—" Then she thought a minute, and said, "There! You see I was *right* to bring my fur coat, and I'm glad I did."

"Where is it?" asked Mr. Jones, looking around at the iron pillars and arches of Benwick Station. "Where are our things?"

Just as they were starting to explain to Mr. Jones that owing to the arrival of Uncle Swen and Auntie Clotilda they were not now needed at the Lines' house, and planned to return to London with him, a very loud voice began announcing something over the station public address system.

"ATTENTION! Attention! Attention! We have reason to believe that a dangerous article, possibly explosive, has been deposited in one of the left-luggage lockers. We must ask all passengers to leave the station at once, in an orderly manner. If you are catching a train, get into it, and it will go. Otherwise, please leave by one of the exits into Rosburgh Road, Glenside Road, or Motherwell Road, where you will be kept informed of events by the police. We repeat: please leave the station in an orderly manner as fast as possible."

"Oh, Pa," cried Arabel in dismay. "We *can't* leave the station! Mortimer's in one of the left-luggage lockers. Annie and Dick put him there before I could stop them— along with Ma's fur coat and our luggage and the picnic bag."

"Ohmygawd!" exclaimed Mr. Jones. He pulled the red-tagged key out of his pocket, went in search of a station official, and grabbed one, who was shepherding people out through an archway.

"Sir! My raven is in one of those left-luggage lockers!"

The official gaped at him, then caught the arm of another, whose uniform was covered in gold braid, because he was the station master. They both stared at Mr. Jones, who repeated, "You can't leave a poor dumb

helpless bird in one of those lockers that's liable to blow up. Think what the SPCA would say!"

Mind you, Mr. Jones thought to himself, dumb and helpless was not really a very accurate way to describe Mortimer, and if the lockers *were* going to blow up, which he for one did not believe, the chances were fifty to one that it was because of something that Mortimer had done.

"You can have three minutes to get the bird out," said the station master. "No more. Go with the gentleman, Turpin."

"What's the number on your key?" said Turpin.

Mr. Jones looked at the key Dick had given him. But the number on the red plastic disk was blurred. It could have been anything from 0000 to 8888.

There were fifty lockers in each row, four rows deep.

Mr. Jones began desperately trying the key in each door that did not already have a key in it. After what seemed about five seconds, Turpin said, "Sorry, sir. Three minutes is up." And he firmly dragged Mr. Jones out through an archway into Motherwell Road.

Only just in time. Behind them they heard a sudden loud whoosh—like somebody slamming the lid of a huge box made of thick blotting paper. And then the whole side of the station buckled outward, with tongues of fire coming through between the yellow bricks.

"Lord—a'mighty!" gasped Mr. Jones. "It really *was* a bomb!"

He raced around to the main entrance, where he found Arabel and Mrs. Jones clinging together with ashy-white faces, while Annie and Dick Line stood beside them, looking, Mr. Jones thought, oddly pleased with themselves, as if they had done something clever.

"Eup. Giggle-giggle. It was us!" said Dick.

"It was those fireworks," giggled Annie. "We put them in the locker."

"I told Annie Dad had got us a box already," said Dick.

"It was to get even with Mortimer for burning my Winky Doll."

"Do you mean to say," demanded Mr. Jones hoarsely, "that it was *you two* who blew up those luggage lockers?"

They nodded several times; little Annie's curried-bean eyes were bright with spite.

"Dick lit the fuses of some of the fireworks, and we put them in the same locker with Mortimer's basket. That'll teach stinky Mortimer to burn up my Winky Doll!"

"Well—if you two did that," said Mr. Jones, "I don't want to have anything more to do with you. Get yourselves home—I don't care how. Come, Martha, Arabel. I can hear the announcer saying something about a London train. We better—" his voice shook—"we better get it."

Annie and Dick walked away, trying to look jaunty. Arabel could hear Dick saying, "Mean old brute. Anyway, I've got enough for the bus home."

The Jones family had a dreadful journey. The Inter-City train sped along toward London at nearly one hundred and fifty kilometers per hour, but nobody had anything to say. Mrs. Jones thought of her fur coat. Arabel thought of Mortimer. Mr. Jones thought of his house occupied by a gang of reckless smugglers at bay, and surrounded by half the police of North London. What would be left of Number Six, Rainwater Crescent, when they arrived in Rumbury Town? Would it be like the wall of Benwick Station, just a pile of rubble?

When they reached King's Cross, Mr. Jones said, "Maybe we'd best go to Rumbury Central Police Station first. They mightn't want us in the way up at Rainwater Crescent if there's a siege going on, if they've got the street blocked off."

Mrs. Jones said faintly, "All right, Ben, whatever you think."

Arabel said nothing at all.

The cab driver who took them to Rumbury Central was one of Ben's friends.

"Heard you had a bit of trouble on your way?" he said, and he wouldn't take any money from Mr. Jones. "What's a ride between pals?" he said. "You'll do as much for me one of these days."

At Rumbury Central Police Station all seemed quiet and orderly. Mr. Jones spoke to the duty officer, who said, "Number Six, Rainwater? The Rumbury Rakes? Superintendent Jarvis would like to speak to you, Mr. Jones. I'll see if he's free."

Superintendent Jarvis was bald and pink faced, but very different from Auntie Clotilda's pinkness. His was the pink that comes from lots of fresh air, and he had a mustache like two white waterfalls, and bright gray eyes. He looked at the Jones family in a friendly way, and said, "How come you heard about the business so quick, if you were up at Benwick-on-Tavey?"

Mr. Jones explained about the gold Mortimer bar, and ringing up Fun-Folks Foods, Ltd.

"So you just missed being first, eh? That was bad luck."

Mr. Jones felt that the bad luck of losing the first prize was a trifle compared to the loss of the fur coat, the house in Rainwater Crescent, and Mortimer the raven. But Superintendent Jarvis went on, "I think I can tell you there will be a reward, though—for the part played by

your, er, family in helping to effect the recapture of the group of smugglers known as the Rumbury Rakes—"

"Capture?" said Mr. Jones.

"Family?" squeaked Mrs. Jones.

"Eleven of them." Superintendent Jarvis counted on his fingers. "Fork O'Farrell. Lee Lombroso. Guffy Quilp. Duke Scodge. Sam Screen. The Tuna. Nosh Mouch. Milly Mantis. Garfield Coral. Pilligreen Lodge. And Open Winkins. All under hatches, thanks to your, er, family."

"Family?" said Mrs. Jones again.

"Raven," said Superintendent Jarvis. "I understand you own a raven?"

Mr. Jones cleared his throat. "Did," he said. "*Had* a raven."

The superintendent shook his bald head. "Nothing *had* about that bird," he said. "Wish we had a few like him in my force. Tackled the lot of them single-handed. With—" he studied a typed page in front of him—"with a do-it-yourself X-ray kit. Your property, Mr. Jones? Not sure if they are strictly legal, without a license, but we'll forget that in the circumstances—"

"I—I'm taking care of it for a relation," Mr. Jones managed to croak out. "But—but I don't quite understand. You say the bird—"

"The raven, yes. What happened was that the gang, having, at eight-thirty this morning, seen, as they thought, your family depart for what looked like a prolonged absence, at nine o'clock entered and took illegal occupance of Number Six, Rainwater Crescent. They needed an undisturbed spot where they could cut a gold bar into eleven pieces."

"Wonder why they didn't just sell it and divide the cash?" muttered Mr. Jones. "They had come by it legal."

"I understand not one of them could trust any of the others to handle such a sale. And they had other things that had not been acquired legally."

"Awkward job," said Mr. Jones. "To cut a gold Mortimer bar into eleven bits."

"Quite. At eleven-fifteen the leader of the gang, Fork O'Farrell, phoned us in some agitation."

"He phoned the police?"

"Asking for help. The raven, it appears, had descended from a miniature infrared oven. One of the gang had lightheartedly switched on the appliance;

the bird was inside and this annoyed him."

"It would, yes," said Mr. Jones, nodding.

Arabel, who had sat perfectly quiet all this time, suddenly turned bright pink and said, "Where is Mortimer now, please?"

"Why, he's at home, at Number Six, Rainwater Crescent, that is, my— Miss; we did suggest he should come up to the station to make a statement, but he, er, declined to do so. You'll find him there—er, PC Halliwell is there too, keeping an eye on the house till you return. I'm sure he will be very happy to see you."

"Then let's go," said Mr. Jones, standing up.

Arabel turned around at the door to say, "Excuse me?"

"Yes, my dear?"

"What happened to the gold Mortimer bar?"

"Well, that's a bit of a mystery," said the superintendent, suddenly looking a little forlorn. "We brought in all the gang without any trouble at all—he had them taking shelter in the larder, the bird did, all—"

"Oh! My Fruity Crumble Cake!" faintly from Mrs. Jones.

"—All but the one who phoned; he jumped out of the landing window and was found on the path outside with a broken fibula. But although we went through that house from attic to garden shed with a fine-tooth comb, not a trace of the gold bar did we discover."

"Oh well," said Mr. Jones. "We know the house better than you do. Maybe we'll come across it; if we do we'll let you know."

"Thank you, Mr. Jones."

The family rode back to Rainwater Crescent in a police car, to the admiration of all the neighbors, who came running out to greet them.

On the ride, Mr. Jones said, "I reckon Mortimer must have wanted to stay at home."

"He wanted to look at Annie's toys," said Arabel.

By the time they stopped in front of Number Six, there was a crowd to welcome them, and a hail of cheers. Mrs. Jones blushed, and bowed to left and right, like the Queen.

Mr. Jones, a bit embarrassed, quickly pulled out his house key and opened the front door. In the hall they found PC Halliwell, sitting, red-faced and stiff, on an upright chair. His right ear was bleeding, quite badly, and he had several tears in his uniform; a button was missing from it.

"Oh dear!" cried Mrs. Jones. "That *is* a nasty ear! You'd better let me put some cream-of-wheat-germ oil on that before you go back to the station. And I'll sew on your button, dear, if you have it."

"Oh—that's very nice of you, ma'am, but I'm not sure where it is," said PC Halliwell. "And I'd best be getting back to the station, thank you."

And he left, very fast, on his motorcycle, which had been chained to the fence outside.

Arabel looked up to the top of the stairs, and saw Mortimer sitting on the banister rail, looking down.

"Oh, Mortimer," she said. And she sat down, suddenly, on the bottom stair, as if her legs refused to hold her up any longer.

Mr. and Mrs. Jones went into the kitchen to make a cup of tea and find out what the Rumbury Rakes had taken, or broken.

Mortimer began coming down the stairs, rather slowly and heavily, thump, thump, thump, until he was on the same step as Arabel; then he leaned against her and she put an arm around him. His eyes were very bright, and he looked exceedingly pleased with himself; as if he had been having a better time in the last twelve hours than ever in the whole of his life before that day.

"Oh, Mortimer," said Arabel again. "Were you in the attic?"

"Kaaark," said Mortimer.

She lifted him and put him on her lap, but he was

too heavy to keep there long; he seemed to weigh a good deal more than he had when she put him in his travel basket.

"You won't burn any more Winky Dolls, will you, Mortimer?" said Arabel. "Ever again?"

"Nevermore," said Mortimer peacefully.

They never did find the gold Mortimer bar; but the reward for the apprehension of the Rumbury Rakes paid for a new hose, and a new doll for Annie, and a new fur coat for Mrs. Jones. When Cousin Ray's collarbone was mended, he came and fetched the computer golf, and told them that Cousin Gladys's new teeth had settled in fine.

MR. JONES'S REST CURE

3

Mr. Jones the taxi driver was taking his family to Wales for the holiday weekend. "*I* dunno what I'm doing. It's *mad* to drive all that way for the weekend," he kept saying crossly as he drove. "Especially in the holiday traffic. I must be out of my flaming *mind.*"

"Oh, Ben," said his wife, Martha. "If you don't get a rest—"

"Yeah, I know, I know. If I don't get a rest, there'll be trouble."

In fact there had been trouble already. Mr. Jones was in such a bad temper that if anything went wrong, from Arabel dropping her apple to Mrs. Jones losing their way on the road map, he flew into a terrifying passion. He certainly did need a rest. There was no doubt of that.

August was nearly over. It had been a long, hot summer, London was packed full of tourists, and Mr. Jones, driving his taxi about the crowded streets, had been working for twenty hours a day for months on end.

"You've got to take a break, Ben," his wife had told him.

So here the Jones family were, on the way to Wales, where they were going to spend three nights in the Sleepy Sheep Guesthouse. Mr. Jones's Cousin Olwen had told him about the Sleepy Sheep Guesthouse. It had recently been taken over by a friend of hers, and was becoming famous as the most restful place to stay in the whole of Wales. "Three nights of unbroken sleep or your money back" was its slogan.

"Worth a try, don't you think, Ben?" Mrs. Jones had said, and Mr. Jones had grumpily agreed.

"If only it weren't such a perishing long way," he said.

The Sleepy Sheep was in a little town called Penny-gaff, among some high mountains, about four hundred kilometers from London.

Mr. Jones had been driving his taxi faster than a rocket for nearly five hours, ever since they had left London at ten that morning.

"Do let's stop and have our picnic, Ben," Mrs. Jones said, every now and then.

"Can't stop on the expressway," snarled Mr. Jones. "There's no place to stop *here*."

When they left the expressway, he said, "Can't stop *there*. Are you crazy, Martha? I can't pull up on a *bend*. Don't be daft, *that's* no place for a picnic. There's houses too near. There's a bull in that field. You can see dozens of people have stopped there, broken glass and filth all about. That's no good, that field's full of turnips. Want to eat your lunch in a field of *turnips*?"

"Oh, Ben! Couldn't you turn down a side road? Then you could park in a gateway."

"There aren't any side roads," growled Mr. Jones, driving at great speed past three left turns. "Anyway, we can't park in a *gateway*. Suppose the farmer wants to come out?"

On and on he drove, while his family grew hungrier and hungrier.

Surprisingly, the only member of the family who wasn't hungry, or even in a bad temper, was Mortimer the

raven. This was just as well, for Mr. Jones was in no mood to put up with any nonsense from Mortimer.

Mr. Jones was sitting in the front, by himself, driving and scowling. Mrs. Jones, with the map, and Arabel sat together in the back. Mortimer was in the luggage compartment behind the backseat. He had himself chosen to sit there. He could climb over onto the backseat if he wanted to, but he did not want to, because he was busy counting his collection of dead wasps. Mortimer had started the collection in London, several days before, and carried it with him wherever he went, in a plastic floor-polish container.

Quite a number of wasps had flown into the taxi during the journey to Wales, for the family had been driving through part of the country where there were huge apple and plum orchards, with stalls of ripe fruit for sale by the sides of the roads, and plenty of wasps buzzing around the stalls. Arabel looked longingly at the beautiful pink and red and yellow fruit as they hurtled past, but Mr. Jones zipped his taxi by all of them at a speed that showed he had not the least intention of stopping. In spite of the speed, a number of wasps had found their way into the car, which had all its windows open because the weather was very hot and fine. The wasps all got blown to the back, where Mortimer added them to his collection. So, for once, he was being quite useful, making no noise, keeping busy, and not bothering anybody.

"Only twenty miles to Llandudno," read Mrs. Jones

off a road sign. "Oh, Ben! Don't you think we ought to stop for our picnic? It's nearly teatime, and we haven't had our lunch yet!"

"Can't stop here!" snarled Mr. Jones. "How can I possibly pull up on a narrow twisting road like this? Use a bit of sense for once in a way, Martha!"

"Nevermore," murmured Mortimer to himself in the luggage compartment, adding another wasp to his collection, which now numbered fifty-seven. Mortimer could not count, but he could see that he had plenty of wasps,

which was the main thing; he laid them out on top of Mr. Jones's suitcase, looked at them fondly, and then put them back into the floor-polish container. Some of them were not quite dead, only stunned.

Mrs. Jones was trying to remember where she had left her glasses. She had half a dozen pairs of glasses, because she was always losing them. She had to keep getting new pairs at Menzies Lenses Suit Yourself Spectacle Shop in Rumbury High Street. But the pair she had lost were her favorites, with red frames and sparkling stones on the earpieces.

"Last time I remember having them was when I got up late to cook scrambled eggs for your father when he came home at two in the morning," she sighed. "I remember putting my glasses on to scramble the eggs— and then I took them off again, before going back to bed. . . . At least I *think* I did. *I* don't know where they can have got to. Do you think I could have put them in the knife-and-fork drawer, Arabel, dearie?"

"No, Ma," said Arabel. "I looked there."

"Did you look in the money box by the phone? I sometimes put my glasses in that, when I'm talking."

"Yes I did," said Arabel.

"How about the fruit bowl? I've dropped them in that sometimes."

"I looked in the fruit bowl."

"Did you look in the toothbrush mug?"

"Yes," said Arabel.

"Oh dear," said Mrs. Jones. "Could I have put them

in the jar on the living room mantlepiece where we keep matches and marbles and Mortimer's old feathers?"

"No," said Arabel. "I looked in the jar."

"I'm afraid this time they're really gone. . . . Did I balance them on top of Grandpa's framed photo?"

"No, I looked there."

"*Ben!!* That sign said only sixteen kilometers to Caernarfon! We're nearly at Pennygaff—and we still haven't had our *lunch!*"

"Too late to stop now. Have it when we get there. Or on the way back," said Mr. Jones, and he put his foot on the accelerator, passing three trailers and a truck.

A new wasp flew into the taxi, and Mortimer stuck up his claw and fielded it neatly. "Kaaark," he murmured happily to himself, "kaaark, kaaark," looking with pride at his plastic container full of furry black-and-yellow bodies.

"*Ben!* There's a huge slate quarry—quite empty—we could stop and have our picnic in there!" cried Mrs. Jones.

"Too gloomy," growled Mr. Jones, scowling at the high, dark-gray walls of the enormous quarry as he whizzed the taxi past it.

"Oh, mercy," sighed Mrs. Jones. "Are you hungry, Arabel, dearie?"

"I am, quite," said Arabel, who always told the truth.

"If only we could reach the picnic, we could peck a bit in the back here. But it's right underneath all the other luggage."

"I know," said Arabel.

"Do I turn left or right at Quern, Martha?"

"Oh my goodness—just a minute, Ben—I've lost the place on the map; have we come through Welshpool yet?"

"Great—*pink*—SNAKES!" shouted Mr. Jones furiously. "Can't you keep your eye on that map for *one single minute*? We came through Welshpool *hours* ago!"

"We turn left at Quern, Pa," said Arabel, taking a quick look over her mother's shoulder. Mrs. Jones heaved a trembling sigh. I can do with those three nights of unbroken sleep too, she thought; instead of getting up

to make scrambled eggs for Ben at three every morning.

At last they reached Pennygaff, which was a neat little gray town, clustered on each side of a rushing, rocky river.

"There's the Sleepy Sheep Guesthouse, Pa," said Arabel, pointing to a white building among trees that stood near the river. "Only it's called the Sleepy Sheep Hotel."

"That's queer," said Mr. Jones suspiciously. "Maybe there's two of them."

"It must be the right one. Why don't you turn down the drive, Ben?" said his wife.

But Mr. Jones insisted on first driving all around the town, in case there was a second Sleepy Sheep. No such place could be found. Finally they went back to the white house among the trees, and Mr. Jones parked his taxi on the tarred parking place at the side of the house. Quite a few other cars stood there already. Arabel noticed that some of them had rude messages written on them in yellow spray paint.

ELLEN POWELL IS THE WORST COOK IN
WALES

GO BACK HOME, ENGLISH PIG!

DAVID POWELL NEVER WASHES HIS HAIR

TOM POWELL RAN OVER ELLY MORGAN'S CAT

Arabel decided not to point these messages out to her father. She thought he might start to worry about whether the spray-paint operator might write a message on his taxi too. And Mr. Jones seemed to have worries enough without that.

Martha went to the reception desk and found that this was the right place.

"It's all right," she said, returning. "They've expanded, and changed the name from guesthouse to hotel. They have our booking and they're expecting us, and Mrs. Powell seems very nice."

Mrs. Jones sounded more cheerful than she had for several hours.

The Jones family unpacked their luggage from the trunk.

"I think this looks like a nice place," said Arabel.

It did. Green hills shaped like pudding bowls rose all around the little town. One hill had a ruined castle on top of it. White waterfalls came catapulting down the sides of the hills. Below, the river burbled among its rocks. I'll go and dam that river tomorrow, Arabel thought. Mortimer will like that too. And we'll climb up to the ruined castle.

"I think you'd better leave your container of wasps in the car, Mortimer," she told him. "Mr. and Mrs. Powell very likely won't want wasps in their hotel."

"Nevermore," said Mortimer sadly.

But several features of the hotel made him forget about his wasp collection, at least for a time. There were two stone sheep outside the front door, for a start. And there was a stuffed heron in a glass case in the front hall. Up by the side of the stairs, one above the other, hung a collection of old Welsh swords, which looked very bright and sharp. Arabel could see that Mortimer longed to swallow them, so she hurried him past them.

The Jones family had two bedrooms, side by side, with a door between and two beds in each.

"Oh, Ben! They're ever such nice rooms! Look at the wallpaper matching the curtains, and all!"

The wallpaper and curtains both had a pink pattern of sheep and shepherds and trees and brooks. The sheep were all jumping over stiles, and the shepherds were counting them.

"Not very good with the windows looking out over the parking lot," growled Mr. Jones. "How'll we ever get a wink of sleep?"

"Oh, but our car's right under the window, so nobody else is going to park there. And Mrs. Powell says nobody comes here late. Oh, see Ben, we can make our own early tea, isn't that convenient."

Each bedroom had a gadget for making hot drinks called a Char-Master. There was an electric kettle attached to a jug and connected to a clock-timer. You filled the kettle, put a tea bag or a coffee bag in the jug, set the clock-timer to when you wished to be woken—and then next morning the kettle switched itself on, boiled, poured water into the jug, and woke you by whistling when your tea or coffee was ready. The Char-Master sat on a pink-and-white tin tray with two pink-and-white china cups, two pink napkins, and a basket full of extra tea, coffee, sugar, and dried milk sachets.

"Better not let that bird get his claws on that thing," said Mr. Jones.

Indeed, Mortimer was gazing at the basket of little tea and coffee packets with deep interest. Arabel and Mortimer had a Char-Master in their room too.

Luckily at that moment the gong sounded for supper and the famished Jones family all hurried downstairs to the dining room. The supper was so delicious that even

Mortimer forgot his wish to swallow the tea bags (at least for the moment), even Mrs. Jones forgot about her lost glasses and the uneaten picnic still in the trunk of the car, even Mr. Jones forgot all his different annoyances. They had leek soup, cutlets baked in crisp pastry, and huge Welsh strawberries the size of golf balls. Just at that time Mortimer's favorite food was pastry (he had a different favorite food every week), so Arabel gave a lot of her pastry to him. He was given a plate of strawberries for himself, and he tossed them up in the air and caught them neatly in his beak before swallowing them—which rather surprised the other guests in the Sleepy Sheep dining room. Then there were several kinds of Welsh cheese, and coffee with mead in it for the grown-ups. Arabel and Mortimer were not allowed to have the coffee or the mead.

"What is mead, Pa?" Arabel asked.

"It's a drink made from honey," Mr. Jones said.

Mortimer did not see why he should not be given a drink of mead. He began yelling "Nevermore, *Nevermore*, NEVERMORE!" at the top of his voice.

"Take that bird out of the dining room, Arabel," said Mr. Jones. But he did not say it as angrily as he would have before supper.

"You can have one run around the garden before you go to bed," said Mrs. Jones.

"Can I have the car key, Pa, so Mortimer can look at his collection?"

"All right. Mind you lock up again and bring the keys back."

In the parking lot Arabel found a red-haired boy with a bucket and rag and a bottle of cleaning fluid. He was busy cleaning the rude yellow-paint inscriptions off all the parked cars.

"Hello!" said Arabel. "I'm Arabel Jones and this is Mortimer."

"Pleased to meet you," said the boy, looking with interest at Mortimer. "I'm David Powell. My Dad owns this hotel."

"It seems very nice. Who writes all those things on the cars?" asked Arabel.

"Well," said the boy, "we can't prove it, for we've never caught him at it, but we think it must be old Gwil Griffith, who runs the Dirty Duck Hotel."

"Why should he write rude messages on your customers' cars?"

"Well, you see, he's mad at my Dad, because my Dad's hotel is doing very well, and taking business away from the Dirty Duck. Everybody wants to come and stay here; we've been full up all summer long."

"Why do you do so much better than Mr. Griffith?"

"Because people sleep so well here."

"Why do they?"

"Aha! That's my Dad's secret!" said David with a grin, rubbing away at an inscription on a Porsche that said, "PUSH OFF, PIG!"

"What a shame you can't catch him at it," said Arabel.

"Ah, he's as cunning as an old weasel," said David. "I have to come and do this two or three times a day. Even so we've had complaints from customers. He comes out of the woods, see."

There was a thick wood of pine trees beyond the parking lot. Arabel could see that it would be very easy to hide in there and dart out.

"I'll keep an eye out from my bedroom window to-night," she said. "It faces this way. What does Mr. Griffith look like?"

"Long, dirty white hair, and very skinny, and his trousers are tied at the knees with leather straps," said David, wiping off an inscription on a Rolls Royce that said, "ROLL AWAY, RUBBISH!" "But I bet you won't see him. You'll be asleep like all the others. Good night, sweet dreams!"

Arabel and Mortimer went upstairs to bed. Arabel was so keen to learn what made the guests at the Sleepy Sheep Hotel sleep so well that she went ten minutes earlier than usual. Mortimer was sorry to leave his wasp collection, and he grumbled all the way up the stairs, making grabs for the Welsh swords—but luckily they were just out of his reach.

While Arabel unpacked and brushed her teeth she was looking carefully all around her bedroom with its pretty pink-and-white wallpaper and curtains; but she could not see any reason why the guests should sleep so especially well. Then she went into her parents' room and put the car keys in the ashtray by Mr. Jones's bed. Mortimer followed her.

"What makes the people here sleep so well, Mortimer, I wonder?" she said.

"Kaaark," said Mortimer, staring thoughtfully at the Char-Master on its pink tray.

"Maybe it's the soap in the washbasin," said Arabel. The soap did have a very uncommon scent, sleepy and sweet, like parsley and thyme and roses and honey and nutmeg all mixed together. And there were bunches of flowers on the dressing tables that smelled sweet too.

Arabel put Mortimer's holiday sleeping nest on the second bed in her room. The nest was really a large ice bucket lined with foam rubber. Under the foam rubber was a Cool-bag that had been cooled off in the deep freeze before the start of the journey. Mortimer liked to keep cool while he slept.

"Bedtime, Mortimer," said Arabel, getting into her own bed, which was very comfortable.

"Kaaark," said Mortimer. And he came slowly out of Mr. Jones's room and climbed into his nest.

Arabel went to sleep at once. But then she always did do that.

Mortimer stayed awake. He was wondering whether to climb out of the window, down the ivy, with the car keys (he had watched where Arabel put them), and fetch his wasp collection.

Quite soon, though, Mr. and Mrs. Jones came up to bed. They were both very tired. Mrs. Jones had a bath, climbed into bed, went to sleep directly, and began talking in her sleep, at the top of her voice. She had been doing this a lot lately. It had been driving Mr. Jones frantic.

"I wonder if I dropped them in the laundry basket," she said. "Do look in there, Arabel dearie. Or perhaps I put them in the bread bin. Or could they be in one of your Dad's gumboots?"

Growling with annoyance, Mr. Jones got out a packet of plastic ear plugs and put one in each of his ears. He had bought the plugs that morning, just before starting the journey, having decided that he couldn't stand being kept awake by Mrs. Jones's sleep talking for one more night.

With the plugs in his ears, Mr. Jones got into bed, switched off the bedside light, and fell asleep lying on his back.

He began to snore at once. The sound was extremely loud, like a pneumatic drill boring through a concrete pavement.

The minute Mr. Jones turned off the bedroom light, a very soft whispering voice began to speak.

It came from under the pillows of the Jones's beds, where tiny loudspeakers were clipped into the mattresses.

"Oh, how relaxed and comfortable you feel! You are lying quite limp, not a stress or a strain in your body. Do you remember the happy days of childhood? Think of them. You are tranquil, calm, serene. Your breathing is slow and deep. Your eyes are closed. You feel utterly peaceful. Your mind is at ease. You have no cares or anxieties . . ."

The whispering voice was talking to itself. Nobody heard it. Mr. Jones could not hear it, because he was snoring so loud himself, and had earplugs in his ears. Mrs. Jones did not hear it, because she was saying nervously, "Do you think I might have left those glasses in my knitting bag, Arabel dearie? Or could I have absently put them on a shelf among the soap in Rumbury Supermarket?"

The voice was whispering under the pillows in Arabel and Mortimer's room too. Arabel was too deep asleep to hear it, breathing peacefully, dreaming about building a dam across the rocky river. Only Mortimer the raven lay awake, listening to the voice that whispered on and on, all night long.

"Remember the happy days of your childhood. Take a deep, deep breath. Now another. You are calm, relaxed, serene. Your mind is at ease . . ."

Normally, Mortimer slept folded into a black bundle,

with his head tucked in under his wing. But as the voice whispered on, he gradually unfolded, until he was lying flat on his back, with his toes and his beak pointing straight up.

At half-past four in the morning, Mr. and Mrs. Jones's Char-Master suddenly shot into action; it let out a high-pitched, ear-piercing, strident whistle, which shrilled on and on, until Mrs. Jones, gasping and wailing, cried out, "*Ben!* Can't you *do* something? Stop that awful noise, can't you? Is it the war again? Is it a nuclear raid? Is it a fire? Is the ship sinking? Ben! *Do* something!"

She gave her husband a vigorous poke with the umbrella that she always took to bed with her in a strange place as a protection against thieves.

"Oooagh!" gulped Mr. Jones, jerked out of sleep, not by the Char-Master, which he could not hear because of the plugs in his ears, but by the poke with Mrs. Jones's umbrella. "Oy! Stop that, Martha! Oogh! What's up?"

Then he took the plugs out of his ears and heard the frightful row that the Char-Master was making.

"Gawd—a'might—what *time* is it, for pete's sake? It's the middle of the flaming night still—what's the *matter* with that flaming thing?"

The matter was that Mortimer, while Arabel was brushing her teeth, had thoughtfully pushed the clock indicator from 8:30 to 4:30.

"*I* don't know what's the matter," wailed Mrs. Jones. "But please, please turn it off, Ben."

Mr. Jones rolled out of bed, staggered across to the table that held the Char-Master on its pink-and-white tray, and pulled the electric plug from the wall socket. The noise stopped.

"*Half-past four?*" said Mr. Jones. "Is this Mrs. Powell's notion of a joke? I'm going back to bed—"

"Oh, Ben, as you're up, and as it's made some tea, do pour us a cup. I'm *ever* so thirsty," said Mrs. Jones. This was hardly surprising since she had been talking without a stop for the last five hours.

But when Mr. Jones poured from the tea jug into the two pink-and-white cups, the liquid that came from the spout was only hot water. (This was because Mortimer, while Arabel was washing her face, had swallowed the tea bag that Mrs. Jones had put ready in the teapot. Mortimer had swallowed the tea and coffee and milk and sugar sachets in the basket as well.)

"*Hot water!*" said Mr. Jones. "I'm poked out of my bed at four perishing thirty in the perishing morning by a perishing steam siren for a cup of *hot water!*"

He picked up the whole tray, cups, napkins, basket, Char-Master and all, and with one sweep of his arm hove it out the open window. There came a crash of breaking glass from below and a cry of pain and surprise from somebody—then a whole series of louder yells.

"Help, help! Murder, mercy, mercy!"

"Oh, Ben!" screeched Martha. "What *have* you done? Perhaps you've killed somebody!"

Rather shaken, Mr. Jones looked out the window. "Anyway," he mumbled. "Whoever's in the parking lot at half-past four must be up to no good—I can't see a thing, it's too perishing dark out there."

"Oh, Ben! I think you ought to go out and see—"

Grumbling dreadfully, Mr. Jones pulled on trousers and a sweater over his pajamas, left the room, and tiptoed down the stairs. He helped himself to a Welsh sword from the wall as he went by, and let himself out through a side door that led to the parking lot. Oddly enough, the side door was already open. Outside, he could see a light flashing about.

"Who's that?" called a sharp voice.

"It's me, Ben Jones—what's going on?" Mr. Jones recognized the voice of Tom Powell, the hotel owner, and walked toward the circle of the flashlight, clutching his sword.

"Hi!" he said indignantly. "That's *my* car! Who smashed the rear window? And who wrote those rude words all over it in yellow paint?"

"He's not far off," said Mr. Powell, and shone the flashlight a few meters away to show a skinny, white-haired figure lying on the tarmac, still clutching a can of spray paint. "But the mystery is, what can have knocked him silly? And why is he all covered with crawling wasps? Mind you, I'm not complaining; I'm very glad he's caught. I'll just phone for the police, if you'll keep an eye on him for a minute, Mr. Jones, and see he doesn't come to and try to get away."

"I'll do that," said Mr. Jones grimly, looking at the rude words painted on his taxi.

While Mr. Powell was phoning the police, Mr. Jones, whose eyes by now were quite used to the dim early morning light, began to realize what must have happened. The Char-Master was lying in the luggage compartment of his car. It must have struck old Mr. Griffith as he was painting the rear window—then it had fallen through the glass and disturbed some of Mortimer's wasp collection.

Slowly and thoughtfully, Mr. Jones took the electric cord off the Char-Master and used it to tie the hands of old Griffith, who opened his eyes and looked around him dazedly.

"Duw! What's come to me, then?" he muttered.

"Don't you move a finger," Mr. Jones warned him, "or I'll cut your head off with this sword."

Old Mr. Griffith gave a groan and shut his eyes again.

By and by Mr. Powell came back with a policeman who said, "Well, I never! The old devil! Well, you prop-

erly caught him red-handed, or yellow-handed, I should
say," and led Mr. Griffith away toward his squad car.

"Best come inside and have a glass of mead," said Mr.
Powell to Mr. Jones. "It's too late to go back to bed."

By now it was growing quite light.

So the two men went indoors and sat in the hotel kitchen, drinking tea and mead, and presently eating hot fresh Welsh baps and scrambled new-laid eggs. Mr. Jones confessed and apologized about the Char-Master.

"I reckon it was our raven set it to the wrong time," he said. "I ought to have thought of that sooner."

Mr. Powell said it didn't matter at all, it was worth it to have caught old Griffith at his wicked work.

"Save us a deal of trouble, that will," he said. "I'm really grateful to you, Mr. Jones."

By and by the rest of the Jones family came down and had an enormous Welsh breakfast. Arabel and Mortimer spent the day damming the river, and Mortimer enjoyed that so much that he almost forgave Mr. Jones for dispersing his wasp collection.

Mrs. Jones spent the day asleep in a deck chair in the sun.

Mr. Jones went back to bed, without his earplugs, and slept for seven hours, with the voice whispering soothing words to him all the time.

When he got up, and came down to tea (with Welsh cakes), Mrs. Jones said: "Oh, Ben! You look ten years younger!"

Next day Mr. Jones took Arabel and Mortimer up to the ruined castle, where Mortimer found a grass snake, and would have started a new collection, only the grass snake got away from him. Arabel was rather relieved about that.

They stayed one more night at the Sleepy Sheep, and Mr. Powell insisted on their having that night free; he was so grateful, he said, to have his parking-lot nuisance caught and stopped.

Halfway along the drive back to London they stopped in a Forestry Commission Picnic Area to eat their picnic, which, all packed in plastic boxes with Cool-bags, was just as fresh as when it had been made. And while she was eating a lettuce-and-tomato sandwich, Mrs. Jones suddenly said, "*I* know! I know where I put them!"

"Where, Ma?" said Arabel.

"In among the tomatoes that are ripening in the bottom drawer of your Pa's worktable. I remember taking them off to catch a wasp for Mortimer."

"Kaaark," said Mortimer, who had got a new collection started.

"Well, I'm glad we got *that* sorted out," said Mr. Jones.

A CALL
AT THE JONESES'

4

It was Saturday, and at the Joneses' house, Number Six, Rainwater Crescent, Rumbury Town, London, everybody was very busy, getting on with their Saturday jobs.

Mr. Jones was busy making bricks out of newspaper. He had bought a gadget for doing this, and he had begun the process of turning all the piles of papers that the family had read during the summer into square lumps of dry, crinkled fuel that could be burned in the fire through the coming winter. The job took two days. First he had to take the old papers apart, sheet by sheet. Then he scrumpled them up. Then he squashed them down into a big plastic dustbin, and poured on boiling water, and stirred them around with a garden hand fork. This part took a very long time indeed, especially as Mr. Jones could not resist stopping to read any interesting news items he might have missed when the paper first came into the house. There were always plenty of these. And then, also, Mr. Jones kept coming across tempting advertisements of postal bargains, with coupons that he had to tear out and put on the kitchen table, so that he could write off for them later.

Mr. Jones could not resist postal bargains. Indeed, it was in this way that he had bought his brick-making gadget. He had also, lately, bought one hundred meters of fast-growing Cape Cod wild-rose hedge, which he had put at the bottom of the garden, ten outsize flannel nightshirts, a rail to hang them on, two folding walking sticks, a giant-size magnifier, an under-bed storage chest, a factory-size can of rustproofing fluid, and an aluminum exercise bicycle.

The trouble with some of these things was that there was nowhere in the house to keep them.

Mr. Jones was out in the back entry, stirring his hot, gray newspaper porridge around and around. Then it had to be left overnight. On Sunday he would ladle it into the brick-making gadget and squish it down into bricks.

Arabel Jones was busy taking empty bottles out of a box and putting them in two bags, which she would then put in a shopping cart and wheel up to the Bottle Bank at the corner of the street. She had beer bottles, cider, squash, tonic, juice, ketchup, and sauce bottles; also jam, honey, marmalade, Bovril, instant coffee, and bath-salts jars. There were two Bottle Banks, one for white bottles, one for brown and green. Arabel was sorting the bottles into different colors. She liked the brown and green ones best.

Mortimer the raven was hindering Arabel. As fast as she put a bottle in one of the two bags, he would take it out again and tip it upside down, to see if there was a drop of beer, or squash, or Worcestershire sauce left

inside. Usually there was not. But sometimes a few drops plopped out onto the carpet, and when this happened Mortimer let out a "Kaaark" of satisfaction.

Sometimes, for a change, he went and hindered Mr. Jones, perching precariously on the rim of the dustbin, and gazing down into the hot, steamy mass of newspaper porridge.

Mr. Jones was not at all keen on Mortimer doing this.

"You go away and find something else to do, my bird," he said several times, threateningly. "Or it'll be Mortimer porridge as well as newspaper porridge, and we shall be lighting the fires with you this winter."

Mortimer seldom took much notice when people said things like this to him. But Mr. Jones spoke in such a firm, fierce tone that, each time he did so, Mortimer would flop off the dustbin and walk slowly away, with his head sunk between his shoulders. But he always came back.

Mrs. Jones was busy trying to tidy the house because Auntie Rita was coming on a visit next day; she was in a terribly distracted state of mind, collecting things together to move them somewhere else, and then finding there was no room for them somewhere else unless she first moved a whole lot of other things, and put *them* somewhere else. In this way she had moved all the brown paper out of the brown paper drawer, where she wanted to put knitting patterns. But now there was nowhere to put the brown paper. She had taken a whole pile of face towels out of a drawer to make room for a bundle of Arabel's summer clothes that were not yet outgrown. But the clothes wouldn't fit in the drawer. And she wanted to put the face towels in a box on top of the wardrobe, but the box turned out to be full of the ten flannel nightshirts that Mr. Jones had written off for. And then she thought of putting the face towels in a box under Arabel's bed, but that space was already filled by twenty oil paintings of Bournemouth that had been done by Auntie Rita on her honeymoon. And when Mrs. Jones tried putting Auntie Rita's pictures in the loft, she found that was full of Plexiglas sheets that Mr. Jones had written away for, and fifty kilograms of colored foam rubber that he had thought might come in handy.

"I shall go de-minted," wailed Mrs. Jones. "I shall go downright desiccated."

She kept losing things, too. She had already put down three of her six different pairs of glasses and forgotten where they were; one pair was on the plate rack above the gas stove, one in a pot of geraniums on the kitchen windowsill, and one pair Mortimer the raven had taken to see if they fitted into Mr. Jones's bedroom slipper, which they did exactly.

Mrs. Jones had scribbled a number of little notes to herself, which she could not read without her glasses, on the backs of envelopes; they were to remind her to order the chimney sweep, get more bleach, mend the tear in the living-room curtains before washing them, dye Arabel's white shoes blue because they still fitted but were getting grimy looking, ask Mr. Jones to clear the leaves out of the kitchen drain, and buy some squirrel pepper for the squirrels, because, if anybody left the back door open, the squirrels came right inside and looked around for something to eat, which they often found. Mrs. Jones intended to sprinkle squirrel pepper over the back doorstep.

The squirrels were busy too. Not because it was Saturday. They were busy every day, collecting all the prickly chestnut cases that kept falling off the big tree between the Jones's house and Mr. Cross's house next door. They carried these cases, with the nuts inside, across the grass

in the back garden and hid them under Mr. Jones's wild-rose hedge. Mr. Jones said if only the squirrels were a bit bigger he'd lend them his wheelbarrow; they were doing a useful job, and they must have sore chests and stomachs from lugging those prickly things across ten meters of grass, and Mrs. Jones ought to leave them in peace. It was a shame to bother them with pepper, he said, when they were working so hard.

Mrs. Jones came into the kitchen to make herself a midmorning cup of Maltyvite. She let out a squawk when she saw all the newspaper coupons lying on the kitchen table.

"Ben Jones! You're never going to send away for all those things! Car blankets! And home safes! And Stackerjiffs! What in the name of Mercury are *Stackerjiffs?*"

"It says," replied Mr. Jones from the back entry, stirring away at his porridge in the dustbin, "it says they solve all your storage problems."

"But where are we going to put *them?*" wildly demanded Mrs. Jones, trying, without her glasses, to read a note she had left herself. It said *Prt grndl Key in mbchck.* "Ben? Did you write this note about the grindal Key in the mobchick?"

"That's *your* writing," said Ben, coming to look. "What's the grindal Key? And where's the mobchick?"

"How should *I* know?" said Mrs. Jones frantically. She looked around the kitchen, which was piled with heaps of face towels, brown paper, knitting patterns, framed pictures, bags of bottles, little notes, newspapers, and prickly chestnuts that the squirrels had hopefully brought inside, thinking the Joneses' house might make a good nut store.

"Have you seen the window-cleaning tool, Ben? I can't find it *anywhere.* And the brush and dustpan. And my handbag. I want to ask Arabel to buy a spool of white thread while she's out taking the bottles."

"What d'you want white thread for now, Martha? I could get it for you this afternoon. I thought you were doing housework."

Mrs. Jones opened the bottle of Maltyvite and found it had gone all caked and hard in the bottom. She began scraping it with a knife. It was hard as rock.

"What do I want white thread for?" she said. "I want white thread to thread the sewing machine because it's

got black on, and I want to do that so as to mend the curtains before I wash them."

"You'd best poke that stuff with a skewer," said Mr. Jones, looking at the caked Maltyvite. Mrs. Jones got a metal skewer out of the kitchen drawer and poked, but the skewer made no impression on the rock-hard Maltyvite.

"You'd better hit it with something," advised Mr. Jones.

Mrs. Jones hit the end of the skewer with a metal mallet. The jar flew into seven pieces, each with a section of Maltyvite clinging to it. Six of them shot all about the kitchen, and Mrs. Jones cut her finger on the seventh.

At that moment the phone rang.

"I'll answer it," said Mr. Jones. "You'd best put something on that finger, Martha."

He went to the phone, which was on the ledge halfway up the stairs, picked up the receiver, and said, "Rumbury seven-o-double seven."

A meaning voice in his ear said, "*I* know who you are."

"O' course you know who I am," said Mr. Jones testily. "I'm Ben Jones, taxi service."

"*And,*" went on the meaning voice, "I know the bad thing you did."

"Here," said Mr. Jones very crossly, "who the blue blazes do you think you're talking to? I never done anything bad!" But the person at the other end had already hung up, with a cackle of knowing laughter. Mr. Jones slammed down the receiver. Just at that moment there was a ring at the front doorbell.

"*Now* what?" said Mr. Jones.

"Could you go, Ben?" wailed Mrs. Jones, who was running about the house with a tea towel wrapped around her finger. The tea towel was starting to go red in patches.

"I've forgotten where I put the bandages," called Mrs. Jones. "I moved them out of the bathroom cupboard to make room for those twenty tubes of bargain toothpaste you ordered and I can't think where—"

She paused and picked a note off the kitchen table and peered at it. It said, *"B & B P in O."* She gazed at it for a moment in bafflement, then went on hunting for the box of bandages.

"Shall I tear up an old sheet for a bandage, Ma?" said Arabel, who had just put her last bottle in the bag, from where Mortimer promptly took it out again.

"No, you see if you can think where I put that box of bandages, dearie. Maybe it was in the fridge," said Mrs. Jones. "I read somewhere that you should keep bandages in the fridge."

Arabel looked in the fridge, and found no bandages, but she did find her mother's handbag.

"Oh, good," said Mrs. Jones. "Now you can go up to the corner with the bottles and get me a reel of white thread at Mrs. Catchpenny's shop on the way back. Never mind about the bandages. I'll wrap one of those face towels around my hand, just for now. Don't step on any of the bits of Maltyvite jar. Where the dickens did I put that dustpan and brush?"

Meanwhile Mr. Jones had gone to the front door. Fred the postman was there; he had a parcel that had to be signed for.

"Wotcha, Fred," said Mr. Jones. "Ah, that'll be my Home'n Dry Martini Cocktail Kit." He signed the slip Fred gave him, and said, "Hey, Fred, some nut case just phoned up and said, 'I know who you are and I know the bad thing you done.' Is he crazy or am I?"

"Oh, I've heard of that chap," said Fred. "I ran into Tom Jarvis, the superintendent from the local police station, at the Peal of Bells, and he said they'd been getting a lot of complaints. This bloke calls people and says things that upset them. Some people are scared to answer the phone, these days. The best thing to do, Tom said, is keep a whistle by the phone and blow it in the guy's ear. That'll soon choke him off."

"Good idea," said Ben. "I've got a whistle, left over from when I was a petty officer. *And* I know where it is. Thanks, Fred. Be seeing you."

Mr. Jones put his cocktail kit, which came in a large box, on the kitchen table, and went to the garden shed to find his whistle, which lived in a biscuit tin with fuse wire, pliers, and insulating tape. He was annoyed to discover that some squirrel had also stuffed the tin full of chestnuts.

While Mr. Jones was getting his whistle the phone rang again.

Arabel had gone out, wheeling her shopping cart full of bottles, and Mortimer the raven had gone with her, very pleased with himself, riding on top of the bags. The pavement of Rainwater Crescent was all covered with fallen chestnut leaves. Arabel had a very good time swishing through the leaves.

Mrs. Jones wrapped the face towel tighter around her finger and went to answer the phone.

"I know who you are, ha ha!" said the meaning voice

in her ear. "*And* I know the bad thing you did!"

Mrs. Jones went into screaming hysterics.

"No you don't, no you *don't*!" she yelled. "You *don't* know who I am! I'm *not* that person, at all! And I never did do that thing! I never touched it! I wouldn't touch it for toasted toffee nuts! I never had anything to do with it, oh, oh, oh, oh, oh, OH!"

Mr. Jones came back with the whistle just in time for his wife's final "oh."

"Why Martha" he said, "whatever's the matter?"

But then he saw the dangling telephone receiver and guessed what the matter was. So he blew a long, shrill blast into the telephone—listened alertly for a moment—heard nothing but silence—and hung up.

"That'll teach the beggar," he said with satisfaction. Then he turned to comfort his wife, who was sitting and hiccuping on the bottom stair.

"Don't take any notice of him, Martha," he said kindly. "It's just some crazy cuckoo. What you need is a nice hot cup of Maltyvite. I'll make you one, right away."

"It's all broken," wept Martha. "Oh, that man did give me a turn! It took me right back to the fourth grade, when Amy Bicknell said it was me pinched the Milky Way from Janice Archer's desk. And I never did such a thing, never, never!"

Mr. Jones led his hiccuping wife into the kitchen, where there wasn't a chair to sit on because they were

all covered with face towels, blue shoe dye, and bundles of curtains. Mr. Jones dumped all these things on the floor and wondered if he should make his wife a quick noggin of Home'n Dry Martini Cocktail. He poured some water on the powder in the twenty-liter jar. But

then he read the instructions on the side of the box, which said the cocktail took twenty-four hours to brew to full strength. "Your friends will be amazed," read Mr. Jones. He put on a kettle for tea instead.

Luckily just at that moment Arabel came back. She had sensibly bought some more bandages and a new jar of Maltyvite as well as the white thread at Mrs. Catchpenny's shop, so they were able to bandage Mrs. Jones up and soothe her down.

"*B & B P in O*," read Mr. Jones off an envelope as he poured the Maltyvite. "You planning to go on one o' them P & O cruises, Martha?"

"Oh, no, now I remember what that *means*," suddenly shrieked Mrs. Jones. "It means Bread and Butter Pud in Oven." She dashed to the oven with a pot holder and pulled out a pie dish of something that looked like boiler fuel. "Oh, *drabbit* it!"

"Never mind, Martha," said Ben kindly. "I never was too fond of bread and butter pud. I'll go out, by and by, and get some ice cream at Saucy Sorbet."

But Mortimer the raven gave a gloomy croak. *He* was very fond of bread and butter pud—in fact it was his favorite of all puddings—and he had watched Mrs. Jones put it in the oven and had been looking forward to the outcome.

He climbed down from the coal scuttle where he had been sitting and slouched sulkily out of the kitchen and into the back entry, where Mr. Jones had his dustbin full of newspaper porridge.

They rinsed the Maltyvite mugs and started getting on with their Saturday jobs again. Mr. Jones gave a stir to his jugful of Home'n Dry Martini mix. Arabel went out into the garden and started helping the squirrels move the chestnuts into the wild-rose hedge. Mortimer moved them out again as fast as she put them in. Mrs. Jones, to cheer herself up, dyed Arabel's shoes all over with blue dye and set them down in front of the kitchen stove to dry. She put the dye bottle into the empty-bottle box outside the back door. Mortimer watched her do this. Then Mrs. Jones sprinkled squirrel pepper all over the back doorstep. Then she sewed up the tear in the living-room curtains and put the bundle of curtains and linings into the washing machine and switched it to "Full Program." A wild roaring and whirling began from inside the washer.

"Ben!" Mrs. Jones called. "I'm fed up with this great vat of derust fluid that's been sitting on the kitchen counter for three weeks. What in the world do you want it for? There's enough derust fluid there to do the whole of Hungerford Bridge."

"I could derust Mortimer," said Mr. Jones. "He looks pretty rusty sometimes."

"I want it out of the kitchen," said his wife. "And I want your exercise bicycle out of the spare room. There's no space to make the bed, and Auntie Rita's coming tomorrow."

"Oh my gawd," groaned Mr. Jones. "That means I've got to hang up all her pictures on the wall, or she'll be offended."

"At least that'll make some space under Arabel's bed," muttered Mrs. Jones, as her husband went around the house gloomily hanging up Auntie Rita's pictures. "Now put that exercise bicycle out in the shed, Ben."

Both the Jones parents were getting cross and tired. They began interfering with one another's jobs. Ben snatched up all the brown paper that Martha had taken out of the drawer and stuffed it into his newspaper porridge bin. She took his giant-size magnifier, folding walking sticks, and foot warmer, and put them just inside the front door.

"There!" she snapped. "Those will do for the Boy Scouts when they come collecting for their sale. Who wants *folding walking sticks*, I ask you?"

Meanwhile Mr. Jones had put his storage chest under Arabel's bed and crammed it full of his wife's knitting patterns. And he jammed the face towels up on top of the bathroom cupboard, where they would be sure to fall off as soon as somebody opened the door.

Then he huffily took his exercise bicycle out to the

shed and rode on it for half an hour, reading the Saturday paper as he did so, and making mental notes of several things to write away for: a set of magnetic screwdrivers, and a clavichord kit, and a waterproof car key and money bracelet.

Then he went indoors for a rest.

"Ben!" shouted his wife. "Change your shoes. I just sprinkled pepper on the step, and I don't want it tracked all over the carpet."

Mr. Jones put on his slippers. *Scrunch*, went the pair of spectacles that Mortimer had put inside his right-foot slipper.

"Martha! Why in the name of blue ruin did you put your glasses in my slipper?"

"I never—" began Mrs. Jones, but just then the phone rang.

"I'll get it!" shouted Ben. "It may be the phone maniac." Hopping with one slipper he made for the stairs, grabbed the whistle, and blew a piercing blast into the telephone mouthpiece. Then he put the receiver back on the rest.

"Mind you do that whenever the phone rings, if I'm not here," he told his wife.

Arabel and the squirrels had finished moving the chestnuts to the wild-rose hedge. (All the chestnuts that had fallen, that is; there were still plenty more on the tree.) Mortimer had moved a good number out again, but his heart wasn't in it; he didn't really care for chestnuts, he preferred chocolate-covered cherries and crispy prawn crackers, so, when Arabel went indoors, he followed her, hoping that it was lunchtime. On the doorstep he paused to test the blue dye bottle that Mrs. Jones had put out, but it was quite empty. As he turned it upside down, Mortimer drew in a deep thoughtful breath; and as well as the breath he also drew in a whole beakful of squirrel pepper.

Mortimer began to sneeze.

"Aaaaaatishoo! Kaaark! Aaaaaatishoo! Kaaark!" All his feathers stuck out like porcupine quills. Birds are not meant to sneeze.

"Oh, Mortimer!" cried Arabel, terribly worried. "Are you all right?"

Mortimer gave her a black look. Sneezing made him feel silly, and he couldn't stand that. He croaked "Nevermore!" in a furious undercroak, and went on sneezing.

"Arabel, you take your outdoor shoes off right away, or you'll track pepper all over the house," said Mrs. Jones. "And make Mortimer wipe his feet."

But Mortimer had already gone off upstairs.

"Can I put on the blue shoes you dyed, Ma?" said Arabel.

"Yes, if they are dry."

Arabel took the blue shoes up to her bedroom, where she found her father trying to stuff the foot warmer, magnifier, and folding walking sticks into the storage chest under her bed. The walking sticks did not fit. So he had to take them downstairs again and hang them on the coat hooks inside the front door and hope Martha would not notice them there.

Arabel went into the bathroom to wash her hands and found Mortimer gazing at the bathroom cabinet.

"Kaaark," he said, meaning that he wanted a black-currant throat pastille. He was very fond of black-currant pastilles; but Mrs. Jones thought they ought to be kept for humans, not ravens.

"Well, Mortimer, you *have* been sneezing an awful lot," said Arabel, and she opened the cupboard to get out the pastille can. Her doing so dislodged the stack of face towels perched on top, and they all fell on Mortimer.

"Nevermore!" he squawked furiously, and he went croaking and flopping out of the bathroom before Arabel could pick up and sort out the face towels. "Mortimer! Come back! You haven't had your pastille!" But

by the time Arabel had the towels tidied, Mortimer was nowhere to be seen. In among the towels, Arabel found the bandage box. Oh well, she thought sadly, Ma will be pleased about that.

While Arabel was in the bathroom, the phone rang again. Mrs. Jones, who was nearest, picked up the receiver and blew a long whistle blast into it. Then she slammed it down again.

Arabel went slowly downstairs, wearing her dyed blue shoes.

"Look at my shoes, Ma! Don't they look beautiful!"

"I did a good job on those," sighed Mrs. Jones. "That's about the only thing that's gone right, so far today." She peered at a note on the kitchen table. *"Blk rdbght Grllfzz.* What do you think that means, Arabel?"

"Perhaps you are reading it upside down," suggested Arabel. She turned it the other way. "Perhaps it's *Zzfllrg thgbdr klb."* They still didn't know what it meant.

Meanwhile Auntie Rita, who lived in Cardiff, was telephoning Mrs. Jones's sister Brenda, who lived in Rumbury Town, not far from the Joneses' house in Rainwater Crescent.

"Is that you Brenda? This is Rita Jones in Cardiff. I've been trying to phone Ben and Martha to tell them I can't come and stay with them, I've got a streptick throat; but every time I call them I get this terrible shrieking noise on the phone. I'm worried to death about them. Do you think maybe there's kidnappers in the house, holding them to ransom? I wish *you'd* give them a call, Brenda."

"Oh dear, you never do know, these days, do you?" said Martha's sister Brenda, and she called the Joneses' number. But all she got, too, was a tremendous whistling noise.

"What d'you think's the matter, Sid?" she asked her husband. "Do you think it's gangsters, like Ben's Auntie Rita says? Or some of those Armorican terrorists?"

"More likely the phone's out of order," replied Sid, without lifting his head from the Saturday paper. "Why don't you call the phone company?"

And then he quickly put on his outdoor things and went to watch Rumbury United play Hackney Wanderers, before he could be asked to do something.

Mr. Jones had also gone to the match, and the two men met at the football ground.

"How's things, Ben?" said his brother-in-law.

"All right," said Ben. "I can't stand Saturdays, though. Too much going on at home."

"Your phone out of order, Ben?"

"No," said Ben, "but—"

Just then somebody scored a goal, so the two men stopped bothering about phones.

Back at the Joneses' house Mrs. Jones and Arabel put on their outdoor things and went along to Rumbury High Street to buy all Auntie Rita's favorite things— shredded wheat and dried figs and bran scratchbread and extra strong peppermints and pickled cauliflower and canned tongue and coal tar soap—all the things Mr. Jones hated worst in the world. Mortimer did not go with them; when they set out he was nowhere to be seen.

"I do hope he doesn't eat the stairs while we're out," sighed Mrs. Jones.

While they were shopping the phone rang several times, but nobody answered it.

On their way home, just as they were passing the house next door, Mrs. Cross popped her head out of the window and called anxiously, "Martha! Martha! I'm in ever such trouble, love, could you be a real saint and help me out, for if you can't I don't know what in the wide world to do!"

Mrs. Jones, who was very kindhearted, said, "Of course I'll help you, Reenie, if I can, what's the trouble, dear?"

"It's Stan." Stan was Mr. Cross, a truck driver. "He's been in a bad smash," wept Mrs. Cross, "and I want to go down to the hospital, but I can't leave Lorita." Lorita was the baby.

"Why, we'll have her with us, that'll be quite all right," said Martha.

"Oh but the trouble is, you know, Martha, how she howls and shrieks as soon as she's out of her own house." This was true. Even inside her own house, Lorita Cross had the loudest lungs in Rumbury Town. Mr. Jones had been heard to say it was a pity they couldn't record her voice and use it for the North Foreland Lighthouse. If Lorita could make that amount of noise in her own home, what would she do at the Joneses'?

"I've put her down now," wept Mrs. Cross. "She only needs another bottle at ten, if you wouldn't mind sleeping at *our* house, Martha, you and Ben could watch all our videotapes, and there's a lovely chicken in the oven, and I just put clean sheets on the bed—oh, I would be ever, *ever* so obliged, Martha!"

Well, of course, Mrs. Jones could hardly say no to that, and just then Ben Jones came home, rather gloomy and out of spirits because Rumbury United had lost their match. He quite brightened up at the thought of video-tapes and the chicken, and said he would drive Mrs. Cross down, right away, to Rumbury Central Hospital in his taxi.

"Oh Ben, thanks ever so, that is really kind of you, I always say, what are neighbors for and what use is it if we can't help one another," said Mrs. Cross, and so Mr. Jones drove her off and the rest of his family collected their night things and went next door and made themselves at home in Number Four, Rainwater Crescent.

"It's a good thing I got all the housework done for Auntie Rita this morning, and we bought the stuff," said Mrs. Jones. "And lucky it's Sunday tomorrow."

Arabel thought it great fun to go to bed in a strange house. She brought sleeping bags and slept on the sofa. The only thing that troubled her was that Mortimer did not accompany them. When they fetched their night-wear and toilet things, Mortimer was nowhere to be seen. Arabel feared that he was still upset, because of

the burned bread and butter pudding, the pepper up
his beak, and the pile of towels that had fallen on him.
When upset, Mortimer was liable to do something dis-
astrous, and then retire to a dark place and sulk it off;
this sometimes took about twelve hours.

Meanwhile Mrs. Jones's sister Brenda had phoned the
phone company, who said there was nothing wrong with
the Joneses' telephone. Then Brenda tried phoning her
sister again. But nobody answered. Then she phoned
Auntie Rita in Cardiff and told her this. Then Auntie
Rita tried phoning the Joneses. But nobody answered.
"That's queer," muttered Auntie Rita. "They're expecting me tomorrow—they wouldn't be away." So she
called Brenda again, and told her she'd better go round
to Rainwater Crescent and see what was going on.

Brenda wasn't keen to do that, in case the house was
occupied by terrorists or mobsters; so she told her husband Sid to go.

"There's nothing wrong with Ben's lot," said Sid. "Saw
Ben myself at the match this afternoon."

"Well, it's funny they don't answer the phone."

"Gone to the movies, very likely."

This did seem possible, but Brenda said, "Well, I shall
phone them first thing in the morning, and if they don't
answer then, you'll have to go round, Sid."

"Oh all right," said Sid.

Next morning early, a whole lot of things happened.
First, Mrs. Cross phoned her house from the hospital
at seven to say that Stan was out of danger; so Mr. Jones

drove down in his taxi to fetch her home. While he was gone, Mrs. Jones and Arabel got up the baby, who was so startled to see unexpected people in her house at breakfast time that she behaved quite well and kept quiet, staring silently from Arabel to Mrs. Jones and back again. They put her in the carriage and wheeled her next door to their own house, for Mrs. Jones wanted to get on with making a seed cake for Auntie Rita and several other things. Still Lorita kept quiet; she seemed to enjoy being in the Joneses' house.

Arabel went upstairs to brush her teeth in her own bathroom and look for Mortimer. While she was washing, the phone rang, and Mrs. Jones blew a loud blast of the whistle into it and put back the receiver.

Arabel came downstairs, looking rather worried.

"Ma, I've hunted and hunted, all over the house, and I can't find Mortimer anywhere. And my feet have turned blue."

Mrs. Jones wasn't too concerned about the absence of Mortimer. In fact, if the truth were told, she wouldn't have minded if Mortimer went away and never came back. But she took one look at her daughter's bare feet and began to shriek. "Oh my merciful cats alive, *Arabel Jones*! You must have caught gregarious gangrene, or gang-blue it ought to be, I suppose, oh my gawd, look at those feet, *look* at them, it can't be frostbite, for the frosts haven't started yet, it can't be the jaundice, for that's yellow, it must be coreopsis of the veryclose veins, oh, *Arabel*, you'd better sit right down on the stairs in case your feet fall off!"

Just then the front doorbell rang, and Mrs. Jones snatched a folding walking stick off the hook in case it was the phone maniac, but went to open the door hoping in a vague way that it might be the doctor or someone who would help in this horrible emergency. But it was only Sid, her brother-in-law.

"Oh, Sid, don't come near here!" shrieked Martha. "We've got something *terrible* in the house. Go away, keep your distance! You'd better send the police, or an ambulance."

Sid, gaping, backed away from his wild-looking sister-in-law waving her folding walking stick, until he was a safe distance off, then he turned and ran. When he got home, he said, "I reckon you're right, Brenda. It must be terrorists. She said, 'We've got something terrible in the house.' I'd better call the police."

"Don't phone them, go round to the station yourself and tell Tom Jarvis," said Brenda, all in a twitter. "Oh, Sid! No wonder when I phoned up all I heard was a shriek. Oh, whatever can be going on in that house?"

So Sid went round to Rumbury Central Police Station.

Meanwhile Mr. Jones took Mrs. Cross back to her own house, and then he went back to *his* own house.

He found his wife in a terrible state of mind.

"Ben! Look at that child's feet! She's got creeping coreopsis! I don't think she'll ever walk again."

"Yes she will," said Mr. Jones crossly. He wanted his breakfast. "And she hasn't got coreopsis. Her feet are dyed blue from those shoes, that's all."

"Oh my goodness, so they are," said Martha, much relieved. "Well I never, aren't you a clever one, Ben, I never thought of that." Then she began to scold Arabel for giving her such a fright. "Go and wash your feet at once."

"I have, Ma," said Arabel. "And it doesn't come off." Now that she knew her feet were only blue with dye, her other worry, about Mortimer, became much worse.

"Oh, Pa, I can't find Mortimer *anywhere*. I've looked and looked, all over the house."

"Oh, mercy Moses!" said Mrs. Jones suddenly. "Could I have bundled him into the washing machine along with those curtains?"

She rushed to the machine and looked inside. But there was nothing except the curtains, nicely washed and dried.

Now Mr. Jones had a dreadful thought. "My newspaper porridge—" he gulped.

"Oh, Pa! Suppose Mortimer went to have a look at it and toppled in?"

Frantically, father and daughter rushed to the back entry. There stood the bin, full to the brim of gray squidge. If Mortimer was under that, he was keeping very quiet.

"We'll have to tip it all out," said Mr. Jones hoarsely. Although he often grumbled at the raven, he was very fond of Mortimer. The thought that the family pet might have been suffocated in a bin full of papier mâché sent cold shivers up his spine. He began to drag the dustbin out to the back lawn, Arabel helping as well as she could. The bin, full of waterlogged paper, was terribly heavy.

When they had it out on the grass, they rolled it on its side.

Meanwhile Lorita Cross, in her carriage in the Joneses' kitchen, began to scream at the top of her lungs. She felt she was being neglected. Also, the Joneses' telephone began to ring. Mrs. Jones picked up the receiver and blew a whistle blast into it. She hardly needed to, with Lorita's howls in the background, but she did anyway.

With frantic fingers Arabel and Mr. Jones were poking and digging through the gray oozy newspaper mush as it came slowly squelching out of the upended dustbin. Soon they were both covered with the gray stuff, and began to look like abominable mudmen.

Just then they heard a tremendous voice roaring through a loudspeaker at the bottom of the garden.

"Put your hands above your heads! You are entirely surrounded by police with guns! Do not attempt to offer any resistance!"

"What the heck?" said Mr. Jones, slowly straightening up. "Resistance? Why the blazes should I offer any re- sistance? Who to? What in the name of murder is all this about?"

A great blue-clad mass of police came swarming over the hedges from next-door gardens and through Mr. Jones's prickly wild-rose hedge. Others burst through the front door of Number Six, utterly dumbfounding Mrs. Jones, who was mixing her seed cake, and making Lorita howl even louder.

Lots of the police had guns. Others had tear-gas sprays, batons, and hoses.

"Surrender!" they shouted. "Come out slowly with your hands above your heads."

Mrs. Jones's hands were covered with seed cake batter. Those of Mr. Jones and Arabel were gray with goo. None of them wanted to raise their hands above their heads.

The police in the garden gazed suspiciously at the two figures doing something with a bin of gray, evil-looking stuff.

"Looks like high explosives to me!" muttered PC Watkins to Detective Constable Murgatroyd.

"Here," said Mr. Jones again, "what *is* all this, Tom Jarvis?"

"Why," said the superintendent, peering through the mask of gray pulp, "that's not Ben Jones?"

"Who the blazes d'you expect—the Hound of the Bakerloo Line? Is this Number Six, Rainwater Crescent, or is it not? What is all this about?" demanded Mr. Jones. "Can't a man hunt for a man's own raven in a man's own dustbin without half the Rumbury police force cannonading into his back garden?"

"There must have been some mistake," said Tom Jarvis. "But what's all that howling coming from inside the house?"

Just then, fortunately, Mrs. Cross came to retrieve her baby. Even so, it took a very long time for the mistake to be cleared up.

While matters were being sorted out, Mrs. Jones made cups of tea for the police force, and whipped up some of her fluffy bran muffins, which she always made on Sundays. As they were all sitting drinking tea and eating muffins around the kitchen table, the phone rang. Arabel was the only one to hear it, as she was still wandering unhappily about the house, hunting vainly for Mortimer. At least he had not been in the newspaper bin, but he didn't seem to be anywhere else, either.

"Hello?" she said into the receiver.

"Arabel Jones! Wherever have you been? This is your Great-Auntie Rita to say I can't come and stay with you because I've got a streptic throat. So you tell your mother, and tell her to—"

"Oh, yes, Great-Auntie Rita, I'll tell her," said Arabel. "I expect she can't come to the phone just now, as we've got the police here." And she hung up, leaving her Great-Auntie Rita so dying of curiosity that she had a good mind to travel up to London after all.

Arabel went sadly back to the kitchen.

"Tell you what," said Mr. Jones, who had just had a good idea. "Never mind all this tea, I've got something here that will warm you boys up." And he pulled out the Home'n Dry Martini Cocktail Kit, which he had put underneath the kitchen table, and opened the box that contained the twenty-liter jug. "Just you wait till you taste this," he said, and took off the lid of the jug.

But the Rumbury police had to wait a while longer before they tasted Mr. Jones's homemade martini mix. For inside the jug was Mortimer the raven, dead drunk, and very peaceful, rolling his eyes slightly, breathing deeply, and just faintly shrugging his wings. He looked very happy. He did not even bother to say "Nevermore," but just croaked slightly at the assembled company, and went back to sleep in the last puddle of martini mix.

"Well, I will be forever blessed," said Mr. Jones, staring at the intoxicated bird.

Arabel drew a huge breath of relief. She didn't mind whether Mortimer was drunk or sober, just so long as he was still alive, and safe with his family.

Just then the phone rang again, and being the nearest person to the door, Arabel went back to the stairs and picked up the receiver.

"Hello?" she said in her polite voice.

"I know who you are," said the person at the other end.

"Oh?" said Arabel.

"And," said the voice, "I know the bad thing you did."

"Oh, but that's not possible," said Arabel politely, "for I haven't done anything bad," and she put down the receiver and went back to the kitchen.

"Who was it, dearie?" asked her mother, pouring more tea all round.

"First it was Auntie Rita to say she can't come after all, she's got a streptic throat," said Arabel. "And then some man called up, but he had the wrong number."